Our Bubble
of Stars

DON'T BRING TOMORROW

BY TOSIN BALOGUN

Copyright © 2023 MoonQuill
All rights reserved.

The characters and events portrayed in this book are fictitious. Any similarities to real persons, living or dead, are coincidental and not intended by the authors.

No part of this book may be reproduced, or stored in a retrieval system, or transmitted in any form or by any means, electronic, mechanical, photocopying, recording, or otherwise, without express written permission of the publisher.

ISBN-13: 9798845630261

THANKS

Tomi, my little rat sister, Toyin, my older rat sister, Aunty Blessing, my older, *older* rat sister.

Deji, my brother, the best one I could ever ask for.

My dad, and my mom, who even when they didn't understand my passions, never believed I lacked the talent.

Mrs. Elena, who made me understand more than anyone else that I could make art, I just needed to find something to say.

Ma. Nina Ilagan, your art captured the soul of this story in ways I didn't know possible.

Dr. Oluyinka Tella, praise from someone of your standing in the literary world meant more to me than you could possibly imagine.

Mrs. Vivian, for being one of the first to think my pen could be used for more than IGCSE essays.

Thanks to Mrs. Evelyn, for giving me an A+ on my third grade English exam.

Thank you, *all of you*.

I love you like fire.

Table of Contents

There	1
Are	16
Too	22
Many	32
Stories	41
Being	50
Told	71
For	78
All	89
Of	99
Them	108
To	117
Have	124
Happy	132
Endings.	143

> We was on the cusp,
> It was holes in the boat, we ain't make a fuss.
>
> —Earl Sweatshirt,
> *Shattered Dreams*

Part 1
For Those Who Would Miss me.

There

"Oh my God, guys. Did you know that rabbits eat their own balls to show dominance? And have you ever thought about how that isn't too different from what men do?" I ask, the stench of whisky lazily resting around us. Placing trust in my butchered motor skills, I pass the bottle in the vague direction of my girlfriend.

"Can't say I have." Momo takes the bottle from me and takes a rather large swig before I can accidentally push it into her face. It's an incredible sight, and I would love nothing more than to express this thought, but Momo says it's wrong for couples to objectify each other, so I only think it. And that makes me feel like a good person, so I try to do a lot more thinking and less talking.

"Ew," Jireh says as she reaches over my chest to get the bottle from Momo. "My brother is sitting right next to me. I don't want to hear about testicles, rabbits' or otherwise.

I hear her take a swig, but my gaze is now locked on Momo, whose very beautiful, very forlorn face is looking up at the night sky. You'd think we'd all be a little more excited, considering we just finished our graduation ceremony about forty-five minutes ago. However, sitting here on the ground in the back parking lot of Myrna Hills High School, passing around a bottle of the overrated liquid fire that is whisky, I can't help but bask in the fact that it all feels so... normal. Despite the fact that we're being shoved out of our childhoods, despite the fact that I have a paper that says I showed up, I keep waiting for the moment when my chest explodes and the choirs of adulthood sing as I strut toward a sunset lined with taxes and impulse buys. But in a way, I suppose life is very much like the whisky Jonah is currently drinking—you see it everywhere you look, but once you get a taste, you realize all the hype was a lie to draw you in and the exit of the bar has been locked.

Yeah, that analogy was fucked from the start, to be honest.

"I think you're overestimating how aggressive rabbits, or I guess guys in general are," Momo says.

Jonah passes the bottle back to his twin, who passes it to me. I grimace, but Jireh shrugs as if to say, "It was your idea, now sip." So I do. Because I hate myself.

"Well I think you're underestimating how much guys equate masculinity to balls," Jonah replies.

I nod in agreement.

As a unit, Jireh and Momo groan and lean away from him, but Jonah just shrugs.

"Jonah, the day the word 'balls' comes out of your mouth again is the day Momo and I commit seppuku," Jireh proclaims.

Momo nods. "That's racist, but I agree."

Jireh turns to Momo and apologizes. "My bad."

A menacing cackle erupts from her brother's mouth.

"Baaaaaalls," he sings, and Jireh glares at him as I pass the bottle to Momo.

"You know, Ayo," Momo says, staring at said bottle. "I love you, but this was a stupid idea. Whisky sucks."

I burp. "It's not my fault. Blame capitalism. Too many options and all that. Consumerist mindset, Macklemore... You know how it goes."

Momo grins and the moonbeams bounce off her perfect teeth and temporarily blind me with their awesomeness. She passes the mostly empty bottle to Jireh, who takes the tiniest sip and smiles like she's done something inconceivably evil when she hands it to Jonah.

He rolls his eyes before clenching them shut and downing the bottle's contents in one go. We all cheer halfheartedly, and for some reason, I get that stupid ball in my throat like I'm about to cry. Not because I feel bad for Jonah and the roughly hundred milliliters of laughably cheap transparent urine he just inhaled, but I think because today just feels so unbearably small. It feels like I've taken a huge step in a pitch-black room and have no sense of how far I've actually gone.

The graduation hat squashed underneath my ass, and especially the godforsaken tassel Mrs. Stacy kept badgering me to turn over, feel particularly stupid now. And the fact that I'm going to Georgia State to get a big, beautiful degree in the collective sigh that is General Studies does a splendid job of aiding that feeling. Regardless, I, of course, don't actually cry. Unnecessary outbursts of emotion rank somewhere above transparent urine on the list of things I hate.

Jonah swallows said urine and furiously shakes his head. Through the cloud of my tipsiness, I try to think of a polite way of telling him he fucked himself over.

"You fucked yourself over, man."

"Yeah, whatever. What kind of depressing-ass afterparty is this, anyway? We just graduated, shouldn't there be strippers or something?" he asks as we all laugh at his misfortune.

After nodding in agreement, Momo stands, brushing the legs of her gorgeous black pantsuit. I contemplate telling her that her suit is hot, since you can't really objectify an object, but I worry it won't mesh with the atmosphere and there'll be that godforsaken lull in the conversation and any attempt at a joke to return the status quo will be butchered when my voice cracks. Which it will. It always does.

I bite my lip instead.

"Come on, guys!" Momo hollers. "We're adults now! We did it! We pushed through the bullshit and made it out alive. We're all going to grab the world by the balls, and that calls for some motherfucking excitement! Wouldn't you agree?" She's too loud, and I fear she might attract some unneeded attention, but the twins seem to soak up her energy and smiles slide onto their faces.

Shit, I'm the only one not smiling. I place one on my face, but they've already moved on.

"Momo's got a point." Jonah stands up, and after cracking his neck, he pitches the bottle at a brick wall a few meters away from us. It shatters upon impact and I feel stupid because I'm the only one who flinches.

After cracking his neck again, Jonah takes in a huge breath, so huge that he bends backwards.

"WE DID IT!" he bellows, something his lazy ass rarely does. His voice seeps into the air and seems to ignite the sky with a flame that stirs everyone but me.

Jireh smiles and cups her mouth with her hands. "WE DID IT!" she echoes, her shrill joining Jonah as the fire builds.

"There we go!" Momo says, kindling the flame with her radiant smile. Then I feel everyone's eyes on me.

"We did it!" I yell. Shit. My voice cracked.

We all laugh at me as Momo whips out sticks of gum from her suit's inner pocket and hands them to us.

"We're all still young and have so much to offer," she begins, "and to be honest, this place was kind of a colossal waste of time for me—for all of us. But at the very least, I'm happy I got to spend it with you losers. Cheers."

We fake a toast with the gum before we unwrap them and toss them into our mouths. And as for her speech, while I love her to death, I have certain issues with it. First, saying that we all have "so much to offer" is a generalization. I don't. And second, the assumption that high school was a "waste of time" would indicate that we all have dreams and aspirations that lie outside of academia, or at the very least have dreams and aspirations at all. I don't.

"That was great, Momo," Jireh says, widely grinning as she folded her gum wrapper and slid it into her purse.

Jonah tossed his on the ground. "Did you practice that in the mirror?"

Her smile widening, Momo shakes her head and shrugs. "Just came to me, I guess."

That's false. She practiced all forty-six words of that speech with me multiple times this morning.

Momo and Jonah sit back down, and I, for some reason, wish I'd have stood up too, if only so I could sit down with them, but then I remember how inconsequential that is. I bite my lip as I look towards Momo who, by the way, makes me wish I was the gum in her mouth. I don't tell her that, though, because—

"On a scale of one to ten," Jonah says, his gaze fixated on a specific star that was indeterminable to me, "rate the likelihood of Jireh still being a virgin by the end of freshman year."

I ignore Jireh's gasp. "Two."

"Really?" Jonah asks, eyebrow raised.

Momo's hands massage my shoulders. "I concur," she says.

The expression on Jireh's face is the literal picture definition of smug, and Jonah shakes his head like he's absolutely done with us. He turns to Momo.

"You concur?" he asks.

"Yep."

"Why do I feel you're just agreeing with him because you're thirsty?"

"I am. But also, let's be honest—Jireh's hot."

Jireh, Momo, and I laugh, while Jonah just rolls his eyes.

I pop my lips, ready to ride the joke. "*I* concur."

Silence.

Jireh raises her eyebrows and uneasily purses her lips; Jonah grimaces, unable to look at his sister. As for Momo, she goes from massaging my soldiers to rhythmically tapping them and doing that motherfucking "tu-tu-tu" thing with her mouth. It takes me a moment, but I quickly realize that I've created another infamous lull, and my stomach drops so low and so fast that it kisses my ass. Heavy beads of sweat prick at my skin despite the night being uncharacteristically chilly, the air suddenly gains the weight of an elephant, and it'll go anywhere but in my nose or mouth. I'm moments, seconds, from popping another lame joke I know I'll regret even more when—

Momo blows in my ear and I squirm and squeal simultaneously. Jireh gushes, "Awww!" and as for Jonah, he rolls his eyes once more and pantomimes gagging.

"He's adorable, isn't he?" Momo asks, like I'm not there being awkward and stomping my foot in the flow of conversation. Like I didn't just make everyone uncomfortable, and like I won't do it again, and again, and again, until and even after they're all sick of me. It's moments like these that make me wonder why they keep me around. Why they tolerate me and all the bullshit tied to my neck that I drag everywhere. Because it's not like—

"The point is," Momo continues, having successfully cleaned up my mess, "Jireh's a catch and she's probably gonna get laid right away."

I try again. Because I have to. Because it has to work this time.

"I'd bet you fifty bucks she'll get laid before her first Christmas in college." Subtly, I hold my breath.

"Hanukkah," Jireh corrects.

"How badly do you want me to pretend there's a difference?" I say through clutched lungs. Jireh laughs and rolls her eyes. I feel Momo chuckle from behind me and I finally exhale. Mission accomplished. Pride restored.

"Oh!" Jireh says, visibly excited. "I managed to get us a double, Momo!"

"WHAT?" Momo taps my shoulder and I lean forward. She gets out from behind me where she rightfully belongs (nope, even in my head that doesn't sound right) and shuffles towards Jireh.

"You got us a fucking double?" she yells, grabbing Jireh's shoulder instead of mine.

The girlfriend-stealer nods excitedly. "It's got a great view and everything!"

"Why didn't you tell me earlier?"

"Because you—"

Jonah gives me a pointed look. "Were too busy giving Ayo your babies."

Momo and I both roll our eyes, but I can't help but think how much I would love to have her babies. Of course, I can't say that, because I'm not a pervert. Or a degenerate. Also, it would indicate how much more space Momo takes up in my head than I do in hers. Then she might dump me. Which I'm surprised she hasn't done yet. Why *hasn't* she dumped me yet? I mean I frequently imagine her with a—

"Ignore him," Momo says, sticking her tongue out in Jonah's direction. "That's great news!"

Oh, yeah... my girlfriend is going to a great art school in New York, and so is Jireh. So they're going to be roomies. Sigh. Therein lies the problem. The problem with everything. Jonah has a publishing deal, Momo is going to be a sexier, Asian Jennifer Lawrence, and Jireh can sing her fucking heart out.

I can whistle out of my nose.

There's just this badgering sign hanging over me that tells everyone—especially me—that in any of my endeavors, I shall be firmly planted somewhere between painfully average and not worth making a spectrum for. Meanwhile, my friends are out there inscribing themselves into the history books.

Also, I lied. I can't whistle out of my nose.

Don't get me wrong, I love my friends more than words can describe, and I couldn't be happier to see them kick ass, but god-fucking-damn, it wouldn't kill me to be friends with someone as useless as me.

Out of the corner of my eye, I see Jonah reaching to rub my knee, but he hesitates, thankfully, and draws his arm back. Every once in a while, he shows his human side to me and it turns my brain into Jell-O. Humans are way too high-maintenance. I prefer lazy-asshole Jonah. That one can fit in my palm.

My expression must be extremely telling, because Momo smiles and says, "Ayo, I have a surprise for you." To which the Eddison twins make "oo" sounds that make me feel important. Well, at least it would if "I have a surprise for you" wasn't our secret code for when one of us wants to speak with the other in private.

Momo ignores them and wraps her arm around my shoulder, leading me out into the parking lot. When we're out of earshot, I tippy-toe and she automatically pulls me in for a kiss. It's one of those good ones too. My knees are wobbling, my ass is sweating, and for some reason I suddenly feel very proud of my eyelashes.

It's a rare feeling that Momo's kisses give me, one of the few breaks I have. Pockets of time where I'm not thinking about how bad my armpits probably smell, or about tucking in my stomach, or that don't know what the fuck I want to spend the rest of my life on. And not for the first time, I wish I could freeze these breaks and put them in a safe. That way, when my friends inevitably do something awesome and it gets bad again, I can whip them out and re-experience this moment. Over, and over, and over, and over... until I have no self to curse at.

Momo ruins it. She pulls away and smiles, rubbing my cheek and looking at what I'm assuming are my eyes. Truthfully, I have no idea. She just licked her lips and I don't know if I remember how my heart is supposed to beat.

"I'm sorry, Ayo," she says.

I blink. "For what?"

After sighing, she leans down and kisses my forehead. When she pulls her head back up, all the pride I took in my eyelashes vanishes into oblivion. Momo's lashes look like God put them there to clean the air whenever she blinks. Her crimson lips, her porcelain face, the straight, draping black locks crowning her head all make her look like royalty. Especially in the pantsuit she's wearing, which looks really... Shit. I'm being a pervert. Shit. Shit. Shit. Okay, I'm not a pervert, look at Jireh and Jonah, they both look great, too. Well, they look exactly the same, but that's not the point. The point is that I admire everyone equally. Which is obviously not something a pervert would do. They're both dressed formally—unusual for Jonah—and their reddish-brown hair is as relentlessly curly as ever. Now that I think about it, they're genuinely attractive people, especially Jonah. Although let's be honest, blue eyes ain't got shit against brown. That'd be like comparing peanut butter to Nutella.

"Listen, Ayo," Momo says, popping the bubbles that are my thoughts. "I just want you to know that while I'm in New York, you're all I'm going to be thinking of. I've even been looking at bus ticket prices, and I really think we can make it work."

I cup my ear. "I'm sorry, could you repeat that part about how you plan to continue worshiping me even when we're hundreds of miles apart?"

Momo smiles and rolls her eyes. "You're such a dork."

Our fingers look for each other, then interlock. "Hey, I feel like I haven't been encouraging enough," I say. "I'm really proud of you. And Jireh, and Jonah. You're all so gifted and it's amazing you've let me hang with you all these years."

She kisses me again, rendering my brain into a little more than pudding. "You shouldn't flatter me so much. And I know it sucks not finding your thing yet, but trust me, when you do, you're gonna grab the world by the horns and then I won't be the only one worshiping you. Give yourself time, Ayo."

I force myself to smile at her speech. I get what she's trying to do, and I love her for it, but hearing someone more talented than you tell you that you'll be like them one day is one of the most condescending things ever. Not for the first time tonight I feel, for lack of a better word, tiny. Like the whole world is taking steps with their giant legs while me and my eensy-weensy ones still aren't sure which path to tread.

Momo doesn't let me bask in my brilliant analogy. Perhaps it's because I really am overly readable, but she can tell her speech didn't do much for me and my very, *very* sizable self-esteem.

"Hey," she says, placing her hands on my arms, "are you taking your medications?"

Blech. So what happened was, in a laughably stupid turn of events, after two cans of beer and the best kiss of my life, I told Momo that I hated looking in mirrors and unveiled the marks on the inside of my thigh. My intoxicated ass was more than half expecting her to feel bad for me, thus netting me another kiss.

Instead, she proceeded to talk to my parents and hooked me up with her cousin's therapist. The saddest part is that when she told me she was going to talk to my mom and dad about it, I relaxed, because they're Nigerian. The only thing that could make a person depressed in their eyes was starvation, and I was one of the few Nigerians who didn't have that.

But no. Despite them hating that my girlfriend wasn't Nigerian—or that I even had a one in the first place—and that the therapist was unexpectedly expensive, my parents agreed. I suspect it was because they thought it would help me decide on what I wanted to do with my life. So the joke's on them... I guess.

Long story short, I'm supposed to be on Zoloft, but it makes me feel like a sleepy beanbag, which is perhaps the worst thing any drug can do. Regardless of that, and despite how much Momo and Dr. Heather refuse to believe me, I'm not depressed. Depression is serious shit. It makes people kill themselves and listen to Earl Sweatshirt, and I wouldn't be caught dead doing either of those things.

Except for the latter.

The point is, I don't take the fucking medicine. I'm not depressed. *I'm not depressed.*

"Yeah, I took it." I say, nuzzling into her neck to hide my apparently easy-to-read face. This tactic has always proved effective, because Momo and I both seem to revel in our height difference. It's perhaps one of the best things about one-on-one time with her—I didn't have to pretend I didn't love being smaller as much as I do.

"Good," she says, running her fingers through my hair. "Ayo, this is for your own good. Keep taking the Zoloft, even if it makes you sleepy. It's not like you don't need the extra sleep anyway. Besides, this way you'll be able to tell me you love me for real."

I pull away; this is new. "What are you talking about? I do. Of course I do."

"Yeah, but..." she tapers off.

"But what?"

"You know."

"I-I genuinely do not know. Like, I am very confused as to where this is coming from."

"Ayo, you've never actually told me you loved me. You've never actually said 'I love you.' And I get it, you know? How can you love me if you can't even love yourself?"

I blink. "What shitty Tumblr poem did you get that from?"

The soft but sharp intake of air and the slight furrowing of her eyebrows tell me that, one, I'm right. She did get it from Tumblr. And two, she's hurt.

"Ayo, I—"

"Okay, I get it!" Jonah's voice rings through the lot as he waltzes towards us. "You want to have babies, but we just finished the bag of dicks that is high school and this is, so far, still a shitty afterparty."

"Sorry!" Jireh trailed behind him, struggling to keep up with his longer strides. "I tried to stop him but he ignored me."

"We all do, Jireh." He reaches us and climbs into the trunk of someone's car. "Anyway, I say we all go to Momo's place, drink some good old-fashioned beer, and I school you fools in Storm. Whadya say?"

Momo fully turns to the twins. "Jonah, Ayo and I were—"

My hand lands on her shoulder. "That sounds like a great idea. Only if you're okay with it, of course." I say the last part with my gaze directly on hers.

The girl I apparently fake-love turns till she's facing me and places both hands on my shoulders. "Are you sure?" she whispers.

"A hundred percent. Sorry I was being such an asshole."

"No, don't apologize. That's my line, I feel like I hurt your feelings, and—"

I conjure up a grin. "It's fine. I'm Nigerian, I don't have those."

She smiles. "You really should stop saying that." Then she spins around and cups her mouth with her hands. "LET'S DITCH OUR PARENTS AND GET WASTED!" Everyone whoops and cheers, finally glad to do something fun for once.

The group and I head towards the sidewalk, and as usual I lag behind them. Momo's head turns back to look at me, eyebrows raised as if to ask me one more time if I'm okay. I nod, and she believes me and turns back around. Either the readability of my face is terribly inconsistent, or lies go well with a little distance and a lot of whisky.

The thing about these people is that I can't bring myself to resent them. They are, simply put, the greatest trio the world will ever see. Just watching them cross the street is like watching a group of Einsteins cure cancer. Each of them brings a facet of information to the conversation in a bewitching harmony that I know I'll only disrupt again if I attempt to join in.

Perhaps the most unfortunate part is that it isn't even entirely their fault that they're stuck with me. The three of them had been besties since pre-school, but then they got lumped in with me for a semester-long science project during freshman year, and I guess they must've had low enough self-esteems to think they couldn't do better than me. It's difficult to describe, looking at the only friends in your life and knowing that every second you spend with them is holding them back. It takes a special kind of selfishness to know that and still have sex with one of them.

"Ayo! What're you doing? Come on!" Momo yells from—oh shit. From the other side of the street? When did they get there? I guess somewhere along the line I subconsciously stopped following them. Shaking my head out of its reverie, I take a step off the sidewalk, over the curb, and my right foot lands on the asphalt as a tired smile finds its way onto my face.

Perhaps it was the change in their expressions. The unprompted contorting from confused but gleeful to pure, unadulterated horror. Or maybe it was the blaring horn, or the fact that time seemed to grind to a halt, as if the universe itself had stopped to watch me make the dumbest mistake in the book.

No, it was definitely the blinding lights on my left, steadily getting brighter and brighter as the truck got closer and closer. The driver barely had time to hit the horn again before his stupid vehicle barreled into me with the force of a... well, a truck.

* * *

I'm not quite sure what happened to me after the collision. I vaguely remember flailing about like a plastic bag in the wind. I probably landed on the pavement a few meters away from the impact point, but I'm not sure.

What I *am* sure of is that it felt like my entire body was on fire. I'm sure I heard Momo and Jireh's screams, and Jonah's "Oh, God!" I'm sure that, moments later, I heard sirens, and I'm also sure that I saw the ghost of flashing lights through my eyelashes.

I'm sure I felt hands on my body, I'm sure my chest traded air for a hot, seething, angry liquid. And I'm sure a gloved, masculine hand was placed in my mouth for some strange reason.

But most memorably, I'm sure I heard what vaguely resembled my voice. Dry, raspy, and broken. Like the words tumbling out of my mouth were jagged and scraped my throat on their way out. My voice, so quiet I doubt anyone but me heard it, poked through my

scrubbed-to-shit subconscious and said, "Wh-wrabbit cht-ch-chtesti-cl-cles..."
   Sigh... Should have laid off the urine.

Are

Assuming there's a limit to how many references one can make to the male genitalia, I'm not quite sure how else to accurately describe what I'm experiencing. I feel the only way to do it justice would be to liken it to that feeling you get when you wake up during the winter. The heater is turned on and the sweltering blanket you're hiding under is in such perfect opposition to the cold America apparently has in its pocket that you somehow find the balls to ignore your mother yelling at you to come down for breakfast. You know you shouldn't, and that one of these days she and your dad are going to follow through on their promise to beat you like they used to, but despite that, the coziness enveloping your body somehow gives you the bravery to do the impossible. Of course, you end up going without breakfast, and lunch, and have to stick with dry Fruit Loops and a melting ice cream sandwich for dinner, but at the end of the day you tell yourself it was still worth it.

That's what it feels like for me now. I can feel people touching me and hear them calling my name. I feel the heat of where the torches are lit glide over my eyes, and I feel my girlfriend's large, trembling hand gripping mine, but something warmer, far more familiar than an ambulance calls me, even if that ambulance has an angel in it. Besides, there's no saving me now. To the core of my soul, I know it: I'm as good as dead.

What calls me isn't so much a thing, but a... a when. A pocket of time that exists outside of my current dilemma. Perhaps a memory? Yes, a memory. One that I've often dreamed about during my worst nights.

We were riding our bikes through Jonah and Jireh's frighteningly large neighborhood. One of those unnecessarily rich ones that almost feel like a town sometimes. It was near midnight, and we had no business riding through the streets instead of playing Storm in the basement. I remember how the breeze funneled around us, and with its overbearing whooshes kept away all external sounds, making us feel like the only people in the world. I can't recall exactly what we were laughing about, but I know our cackles had a certain spark in them. I might be mistaken, but I'm pretty sure that was the day Jonah got accepted by a literary agent, about two weeks before summer break would officially end and we'd become seniors.

Their excitement seemed so contagious that the air around us felt lighter, like it, too, was laughing with us. Everything seemed to be one big joke back then, and the stars smiling down at us were in on it. With Momo's hair riding the breeze and Jireh and Jonah yelling words that seamed into it, I smiled wider than I had in a long while. It was one of those moments where it just felt good to exist.

"WHOOHOOOO!" Momo whooped at the top of her lungs, and her excitement infected me with the same glee the night had. We had to have been riding for about thirty minutes by that point; our legs burned and our lungs seemed unable to get quite enough oxygen, but that wasn't what stopped us.

We got to the small park at the center of the neighborhood, and under the massive, dusty Oak Tree, the same one Momo told me she loved me and kissed me under, sat a man wearing a rumpled, piss-yellow, garbage collector uniform. His neck was awkwardly slumped, clods of foamy saliva dripped down his mouth, and in his arm was what we later found out to be a broken syringe needle. In an instant, the wind and the stars stopped laughing and our bubble of cackles and sweat popped. We were no longer the only people in the world, and I'm not sure, but I think Jireh gagged before she turned away.

The rest of us just stared at the man, mouths agape in a blend of fright and sorrow. His stubble was unkempt, his hair a ravaged bird's nest, his skin a hollow mountain range, and his bloody nails had been scratched to shit. Back in Nigeria I had seen starving kids everyday on the way to school, the mentally ill walking naked through main roads, and elderly people sleeping in bushes, but I still don't think I had ever seen such a depressing image.

"He's not breathing," my voice said.

As if she had snapped out of a trance, Momo jumped, then frantically pulled her phone out of her back pocket. I wasn't looking at her, but I could hear the sound of her screen-tapping, of the "Nine-one-one, what's your emergency?" and of her frenzied report constantly interrupted by her panting. Which I knew wasn't because we'd just ridden for half an hour.

Jonah took my hand, and I didn't pull away. I let him hold me as my girlfriend took charge of the situation. Together, we stared in heavy silence for what must have been several minutes, until the sound of overlapping sirens tore through the air and Jireh pulled her brother into a hug. His fingers left mine, but I still fixed my gaze on the man. Something about his eyes kept me from looking away. He looked tired. Even in death, he looked like he just wanted a good night's sleep. As if the bullshit shoved down his throat still choked him even after he vomited it out. The outer tendrils of my mind had just about crawled to the thought of whether or not there was a point to living at all if not even death could count as rest when I felt the firm hand of a police officer on my shoulder.

She pulled me away and told me to join my friends sitting on a bench a few meters to our right as her team began wrapping yellow tape around the scene.

When I met up with the others, everyone had a different glint in their eyes. Momo's reflected a fabricated strength. She couldn't break down, because then *we* would break down. So she resorted to biting her lip and blinking away tears. Jonah, on the other hand, made no move to hide his shock. His wide eyes looked bigger than golf balls and he just kept gulping, and gulping, and gulping. As for Jireh, I couldn't see her eyes through the tears, but it wasn't exactly hard to tell how she was feeling.

Taking a large gulp of my own, I sat down next to Momo and did nothing but breathe for a while.

"So, rough night?" I joked in a feeble attempt to kill the gloom resting on our shoulders.

Jonah didn't even bother to look my way when he said, "Shut up, Ayo."

So I did. I specifically remember biting the inside of my cheek as punishment for my stupidity. I bit it even more when I turned to Momo and saw she was shaking her head at me, her eyebrows furrowed in distaste. My gaze fell to my feet.

Jireh, her lips still quivering, turned to her brother. "Jonah, Heaven and Hell... it's still there, right?"

Unlike with me, he looked at her, and when he saw how shaken up his sister was, he employed the same forced strength Momo had and cleared his throat. "What do you mean?"

"I believe what Rabbi Davis says, really I do, but seeing an actual dead body feels... it feels silly. Heaven and Hell feels silly now. Like... like playtime's over. 'Cuz, I mean I could... I could touch him. I could reach out and touch him. If his soul is in Heaven or Hell, I don't know, but I-I can't touch that. That can't hurt, but he can..." she whispered, hugging herself.

I didn't say anything, but I agreed with her. While I had never clung that tightly to what I was taught in church, the image of the dead man that was burned into my retinas didn't match with the golden gates nor the flaming pools filled with strippers and homosexuals. The only image that felt right for something like this was... dirt. Ugly, dry, pale-faced, foam-mouthed dirt.

"I hope there is," Jonah said, holding her hand. "God, I hope there is."

"If there is, we're all going to Hell," Momo said with a humorless snort.

Everyone seemed to have dropped the no-joke policy as Jonah and Jireh jadedly chuckled. I remember giving a laugh in tandem, but knowing me, it was probably too loud and too late.

"What if it's nothing?" I said without thinking.

No one said anything in response, and I know it's because I disrupted the flow that Momo had just managed to stabilize, but I took it as an invitation to continue.

"What if we die and it's like sleeping, only there's no more days to wake up to? It's just nothing, and everything we love might as well not exist. The entire world might as well not exist. And that man, did that man really exist? Did he fulfill his dreams?"

I was beginning to sound a little manic by that point, but didn't harbor any desire to stop. "Did he even *have* any dreams? What if he's just a percentage now? What if that's all he'll ever be? A ticked tally mark. How many people were affected, even a little, by his existence? How many will remember him? What even *is* he? Does he count a person? I mean"—I sniffed—"I mean, if you can slip through the cracks that easily, did you even really exist in the first place? Was there a point to it all?"

I wanted to continue, but chose then to shut up because I sounded stupid as fuck and my voice had cracked at the word "remember."

For a few beats, the only sounds that could be heard were of trees rustling, the occasional cricket, the police officers talking to each other, and the humming of their car engines.

"I will." Jireh sniffed and cleared her throat. "I'll remember him."

Jonah's grip on his sister's hand tightened. "Me too," he said.

Standing up and brushing her jeans, Momo turned to us and forced another smile. "Me too."

I knew everyone was looking at me, but my mind wasn't on that. It was on the fact that, that day, I had seen real depression. I had seen the kind of sadness that doesn't give you a break even after you die. The marks on my thigh and the voices in my head telling me I'm worthless were nothing. My "depression" was nothing. Momo, and all her self-righteous declarations of aid were nothing.

It was then that I decided to stop taking the damn Zoloft. After which I finally raised my head to see Momo worriedly looking at me. For the first time in a while, the words that left my mouth didn't stem from the fact that everyone else was speaking, but because I meant it, from the bottom of my soul to the tips of my fingers. Like Momo, I forced a smile.

"Me too."

Too

I never realized this before, but waking up in a white space, with no perceivable walls, or up or down or left or right or anything, just an endless sea of blankness, is no different from walking with your eyes closed. I have no idea if I'm falling or lying on my back, all I know is that if this is Heaven, it's underwhelming, and if it's supposed to be Hell, it might as well be Heaven.

It's weird, though. I think I might be lying on something, but turning over has revealed more white stretching on forever. The feeling of pressure I should only have on my back is evenly distributed to almost every inch of my skin, such that it's hard to tell if I'm lying on my face or my side.

"Oh! He's awake!" a soft, male voice says from what I guess is my right.

"He's been awake for a while now. Lazy bastard just doesn't want to get up," another voice says.

This voice sounded harder; each syllable sounding like they were being forced to be here and wanted nothing more than to go home.

I'm not sure how, but I manage to stand, I think. For all I know, maybe I've mastered the headstand. A few meters ahead of me, two boys are staring at me. The one on the right is wearing a sky-blue sweater over a white shirt and khakis and looking at me with a warm smile.

As for the one on the left, he exudes worrisome amounts of Wattpad-love-interest-aura, with his obscure band t-shirt and leather jacket with jeans. All black. Definitely not sexy. Because I'm eighteen years old. And eighteen-year-olds don't find Wattpad love interests sexy. That's ridiculous, even if his edgelord jeans do look kind of nice.

Thinking of clothes (not his specifically, of course) makes me look down at mine, and it takes me a few seconds to realize what I'm staring at.

It's my penis.

Ah! It's my penis!

Before I have time to cover my appendage, the boy in the sweater starts to walk towards me, or perhaps sliding on his head towards me. The details remain unclear at this moment.

"I apologize, your natural state in this plane is without clothes. Here, let's fix that."

He flicks his fingers and nothing happens, then I follow his gaze and—HOLY SHIT! Somehow, where my stomach rolls used to be is a white t-shirt and a white pair of shorts.

"What the fuck?!" I squeal, because whenever I'm frightened, my voice always decides how it wants to sound without asking me first. "Who the hell are you guys? Where am I? Are these clothes real?"

I'm picking at my clothes to see if they'll disappear upon contact when the Wattpad fuckboy rolls his eyes and says, "Jesus-fucking-Christ, man. You're dead. Calm down."

I blink. "Pardon?"

The one clad in the sweater rushes to diffuse the situation. "W-well, what my associate is trying to say is that you were in an accident and, well, you're currently fighting for your life in a hospital."

Oh yeah. The truck. "Well, am I gonna be okay?"

The sweater guy opens his mouth to respond but the other interrupts him. "You're here, so no. You are one hundred percent fucked."

Once again, my body acts without asking my permission. This time, it's my knees that give out before the fact that I'm dead even has the chance to fully reach my brain.

Holy shit. I'm dead.

Thump. Thump. Thump.

I'll never find out what I want to spend the rest of my life doing. I'll never touch Momo again. Never apologize for being such a drag on her life. My parents won't be able to finally see me make them proud. It stacks and it stacks and it stacks, getting more focused and harder to swallow with each closed door.

What aches the most isn't even that I'm needed by no one, or that I didn't get to die as someone who mattered, but that I didn't even get the chance to find the tools to *make* myself matter. Instead, I died as "that guy"—the one that everyone has in their friend group, the one who ceaselessly copied his girlfriend's homework and bitched his way out of any form of responsibility.

Thump. Thump. Thump.

The weight of all that I'll never get to accomplish leans against me with what must surely be enough force to break my spine, and my lungs shrivel up and refuse anymore oxygen. My fingers quake as cold beads of sweat pour out of my skin in droves. And, as if it's sad to miss out on the fun, my stomach shrivels, too, shoving all of its content out onto what I can only assume is the floor. A revolting, moist squelching sound resonates upon impact.

Thump. Thump. Thump.

Then, for a moment, my entire being—from the tips of my fingernails to the banks of my vomit pool—feels like it's someone else's. Like I'm watching myself from a drone. Disgust, thick and acidic, wells up in my gut at what I see. It's bitter and potent that I almost want to vomit again. Of course I'm dead. Life was a gift, and from the moment I was born, I never once bothered to unwrap it.

Thump. Thump. Thump.

The sweater guy is trying to talk to me, but the *thump, thump, thump* of my pulse drowns out his voice. I can't hear him, and I don't want to hear him. I just want nothing, just silence. Just silence.

Except, I suppose I do have silence, now more than ever, when I'm in an empty space, separate from everything that once hurt me. The only problem is that it's the loudest thing I've ever heard. Louder than my pulse, louder than my panting or the *splat* of my vomit projectile. Louder than any noise I could've possibly made when I was still alive.

I heave and vomit what's left of my stomach contents as my mind wanders back to the man under the oak tree. I didn't understand why he still looked tired back then, but I get it now. There's no such thing as peace, only the screaming realization that you're the dumbass who died jaywalking. And now you'll be less than a blip in the story of humanity.

My chest relaxes, and oxygen rushes back into my lungs. It all happens so fast that it takes me a minute to realize the hurt is gone.

Then, silence.

"What?" I croak to no one in particular. It's an indescribable feeling. Because I know I'm dead, but for some reason I can't bring myself to ache over it anymore. The sensation of all the sadness and despair being sucked out of me is such a novel experience that I can only liken it to how I think balls feel at the tail end of a blowjob. I almost want to cry, but my body won't let me.

The leather-clad Wattpad fuckboy groans. "Goddamn it, man. You should've let him feel it for a little longer." He's looking at his companion, who has his fingers positioned in a way that tells me he just flicked them.

"I... I'm beyond confused," I admit, biting my lip.

"Well, to put it plainly, you're in the afterlife, and me and my friend here are essentially... gods? Yes, gods. That's the easiest way for me to explain it to you," Sweater Guy says.

My eyebrow raises against my will. "God wears a leather jacket?"

The guy in leather rolls his eyes. "Our bodies adjust to your culture, dumbass."

"You're rude."

"And you're a dumbass."

"Still rude."

"Still died jaywalking."

"That's fair. So you said I'm dead?" I turn to Sweater Guy, "Why aren't I crying anymore?"

"Please don't be mad, but I tampered with your brain just a little, so you don't feel that dread anymore. You'd be surprised how many humans spend eternity in a loop, lamenting over what-ifs."

"You... removed some of my emotions?" I ask.

The guy, who's apparently *God*, mind you, looks pensive. "Well, yes. But I promise I only did for your benefit. You see I—"

"Awesome!"

"—really just want the best for—wait. What was that?"

"Awesome."

"Oh."

"Emotions like that would probably just get in the way," I say.

"Something we agree on," Leather Guy says, hands tucked in his pockets because why the hell not.

"Sorry. I've been referring to you guys as Sweater Guy and Leather Guy in my head," I explain. "It would really help if I knew your names."

The two look at each other, and their expressions tell me this is something that happens to them quite often. Sweater Guy is the one who speaks up.

"Since our names would be physically impossible for you to pronounce, you can give us whatever names you want."

"Except for God. Don't call us God," deadpans Leather Guy.

Sweater Guy nods. "We personally find that term a little reductive."

I don't know why I'm not pissing my pants, these two are literally the creators of the universe... I think. Regardless, I chalk my bravery up to Sweater Guy messing with my brain as I point at Leather Guy. "God One," I say. Then I point at Sweater Guy. "God Two."

God One's eye twitches. "Listen here, you little shit. I could blink and you'd be reduced to a strand of hair on my fucking ballsack, so don't fuck with me, you goddamn—"

"What he's trying to say is that, while we do find it unnecessary, we acknowledge and are grateful for the names," God Two intervenes.

"What? No! I'm saying that—"

"That this is just one instance of the hundreds of billions of projections of ourselves and we don't mind a few humans calling us 'God', right?" he says while looking at God One with a surprising amount of spunk.

God One huffs. "Whatever."

"Anyway," God Two says, perking up, "welcome to what you would call the afterlife! Here you can view the complete story of humanity—past, present, and future—for all of eternity!"

"Or until you want us to crush your soul," God One adds with perhaps too much enthusiasm.

"W-well, yes. That is on the table, but there is so much to see! You could visit King Tut during his reign, or perhaps you would like to see if humanity overcomes the climate crisis?"

God One fishes a lollipop out of his pocket and puts it in his mouth. "Spoiler: they don't."

"I figured," I say.

God Two continues, clearly not glad to be the only excited one. "Regardless, there's a procedure that precedes all that." He clears his throat. "Ayo Aluko, would you like to see your last moments?"

"Uh... yeah, sure," I reply, still waiting for my entire situation to fully sink in, whenever that happens. *If* it happens. I really hope it doesn't, because I—

God Two snaps his fingers and the scenery changes. My surroundings switch from a never-ending plane of white to a beige hospital room. The change is so sudden that my feet, forgetting what it's like to have solid ground to stand on, lose balance and I topple over like a vase.

Being a gentleman, God Two helps me up while the other one just stuffs his hands into his jeans pockets and snickers.

The room is fairly standard. The walls are barren, there's a window on the right side giving way to the night sky, and two navy-blue chairs by the door.

God Two gestures to a large bed in the corner. Surrounding it are an innumerable measure of machines strapped to the still, battered body on the mattress. I don't want to move forward, because I know I'll recognize myself. Underneath the broken body parts and the beeping monitors, I'll see my stupid chipmunk cheeks and sausage fingers. And when that happens, it'll hit me on a whole new level.

My body seems to get a kick out of acting without asking, though, because it trudges forward, moving closer and closer to a hideous, good-as-dead version of myself.

If it weren't for God Two's influence, I'm almost certain that the torrent of vomit would rear its slimy head again. Lying on the hospital bed in front of me is... not me. It's an edition of me. One with friends and a girlfriend who's way out of his league. One who's not inconceivably and cosmically alone. And he's dying. He's also worryingly ugly, with swells of flesh that go inches high and blotches of skin that are way too red and way too blue for comfort. It almost looks like someone dipped a large spoon into my face and swirled it like soup. My eyes, nose, and mouth don't look like they're where they're supposed to be.

Perhaps because I'm so focused on myself at the moment, it takes a moment for my mind to register my friends and parents moving towards my body through my peripherals. Like suicidal moths to a flame, they gradually gather around my broken body. When it becomes clear just how fucked up I am, as if on cue, Momo, Jireh, and my mother burst into heavy sobs, each one pumping through their bodies, quaking them like a live wire. Or a heartbeat.

"You okay?" God Two asks.

I jump when he says this, as I had completely forgotten he was here. Though I doubt my face agrees with me, I nod and turn back to my people.

Slowly, with fear spiking in every step, I walk over to them and try to place my hand on Momo's shoulder. It ripples through her like she's made of water. Like I'm Obito or some shit. And while I'm sure Alive-Ayo would've thought that was awesome, Dead-Ayo blinks away tears.

Momo's trembling fingers wrap around dead-me's, and when she squeezes, she manages to conjure up one of her award-winning fabricated smiles. It's feeble now though, constantly dropping into a grimace before leaping back over the surface into a smile.

"You're going to be okay, Ayo," she lies. "The doctors are gonna fix you right up. It'll be like... like it never happened." Her lips have surpassed her hands in their quivering but she still lets go of my fingers when she sees the look on my dad's face.

A doctor appears out of thin air and places his hand on my mother's shoulder. He says something in her ear, and her shoulders somehow manage to shake even more. My mother. *My* mother. The woman who used to beat me with whatever tool she had on hand. The one who, when I got lost in Six Flags, calmly waited at the restaurant and took away my PS Vita when a police officer brought me to her. The one who sold my laptop and phone on the day I forgot to set up her iPad. Simultaneously the nicest and most unpleasant person to tread this earth.

This baffles me. I'm not saying I don't know why she's crying. I obviously know my parents love me. They might not be the best at showing it, but that's a just a trait the three of us, and quite honestly, most Nigerians share. However, to see her cry like this, it feels... like the man. The man under the tree. It doesn't feel like love, or even sadness or any other needlessly intangible concept. It feels like dirt and makes me feel sick to my stomach again.

I see a moving object in my peripheral, so I follow it to see a man in a dead-gray hoodie, ratty jeans, and a muddy green beanie. He's hunched over and weeping almost as hard as my mother is. On the chair, just outside the room, he's rocking back and forth, his fists clenched so tight around the sides of his head that I worry they might burst.

A clump forms in my throat as I fruitlessly ask, "Who's that?"

God Two blinks. "W-well, uh... that's—"

"The guy who killed you," God One says without a hint of snark in his voice. "That's the man who killed you. Joshua Williams."

It didn't sound like he was saying it to me. Rather, it felt more like he was proclaiming it to everyone and everything. Like he was stitching—no—ramming his will into the very fabric of the universe.

Many

On my first day of school in America, I stood by the field during recess and watched the entire school run around screaming like a bunch of animals. That's what I called them in my head back then—animals.

In truth, I envied them. I wanted more than anything to be an animal. To not be so aware of myself that I could run around with wild abandon, go up to anyone I found interesting, and ask them if they wanted to be my friend, as fourth graders so often did. But I couldn't. I stood there and watched others enjoying themselves. Eventually, I'd just walk back to the classroom and wait for the break to end, thinking over and over again, *I don't belong here. I don't belong here.*

Back then, I blamed it on the fact that I was Nigerian, and therefore couldn't operate on quite the same frequency as everyone else, but even my ten-year-old brain knew the truth. Even back in Nigeria, it always felt like there was a glass wall between me and everyone else. Whenever I tried to talk to someone, my voice would come out muffled, like it wasn't quite mine. And I could see it in their eyes, the light leaving as they quickly lost interest in the mumbling idiot with the perpetual voice cracks.

Now, though, in a hospital room with my battered body laying a few meters away from me and my killer blubbering to my father, the glass wall feels a thousand times thicker. Whatever melodramatic responses I had to hanging out with people who might as well have spoken a different language pale in comparison to seeing Momo cry. And it hurts more because it's not even a sad cry, like the kind you see in funeral scenes in movies or when something sad happens in a book. Momo's weeping is the kind that bursts out when you're in pain, when you break a bone or get a door slammed on your thumb.

Ugh. This is all wrong. And it's all my fault. I should belong here. *I should belong here.*

"I-I'm really sorry!" the man says to my dad. "I swear he just popped out of nowhere. By the time I hit the brakes, it was too late! I swear I—"

"Shut up!" Momo cries, pointing a quivering finger at his face. "You were going way too fast and you know it! Don't act for a second like you're not the one responsible!"

"Okay, maybe I was a bit over the speed limit, but I swear, he really just popped out of nowhere! If he hadn't, I honestly wouldn't have—

Jonah doesn't let the asshole finish. He grabs him by the collar, his grip so tight I fear his fist might snap.

"The bottom line is," he growls through clenched teeth, "if you had followed the fucking law, Ayo would be fine. But now you can't fix it. YOU CAN'T FIX IT!" Jonah shakes the asshole back and forth with so much venom that his ratty beanie falls off.

It goes without saying, but I've never seen Jonah like this. I thought he was like me in that he just didn't have it in him to react this way. I never knew he cared that much. Fuck. Why didn't he ever tell me he cared that much?

Why didn't I let him?

"Listen man," the asshole says, pushing Jonah away, "everyone goes over the limit! Everyone! I'm not the one out of the ordinary here!"

Jonah says nothing, and it's probably because he knows the asshole has a point.

"So I was just doing what everybody does every day, and he was the one out of line, not me! Not looking both ways and just stepping out onto the sidewalk like that? Come on!"

Silence.

"Look, I'm really sorry. Really, *really* sorry. But you've gotta understand that—"

With a speed no one knows she had, my mother dashes up to the man and slaps him across the face. The beeping and booping of the machines show no signs of halting, but the sound of the impact is so sharp and resolute that it feels like it silences the entire hospital.

"How dare you?" she says, the vein in her forehead bulging. "When you do something so horrible, you take responsibility! Yet here you are—"

"What's your name?" my dad asks. It's the first words he's said since they had arrived. His voice lacks its usual boom, but it's still as unwavering as ever.

"J-Joshua, sir," the asshole replies.

Slowly, my dad walks up to him, maintaining eye contact. When he's about a foot away from Joshua, he stops and deeply sighs. It's almost like he deflates, his large body losing all of its rigid masculinity. With one exhale, he looks like a shell of his former self.

Tired. He looks fucking tired.

"If we were in Nigeria, you wouldn't be breathing right now." His voice cracks. *Oba Aluko's* voice cracks. "But I understand."

The silence is even louder now, and for a moment, I'm wondering why. Then it hits me. His words settle in my brain and it hits me.

Momo copy-and-pastes my thoughts before I can say them. "You understand? What do you mean?" Her voice is dangerously composed.

"Ayo has always struggled with leaving his head and being aware of his surroundings." It's obvious he's talking to Momo, but from the way he doesn't look at her, or the break he took before answering, it still feels like an insult. My blood boils and my fists don't ask me before they clench, nor does my heart before it pounds against my in my ears. I can't fucking believe him. I can't *fucking* believe him! He and I never saw eye to eye, but for God's sake it wouldn't kill him to just be angry for me! I'm dead! I'm fucking dead and all he has to say is "I understand"? Judging from everyone's expressions, the only person who's angrier than Momo and I right now would probably be—

My mother slaps my father.

From the look on her face, it stuns even her. In our culture, especially of the Christian variation, men and women have fairly distinct places in a relationship. And a lot of women, including my mother, accept it without a hint of opposition. For that reason, I suspect that for her, the slap was to her own face as well.

Slowly, like his hand is made of lead, my father brings his palm to his cheek and turns to my mother. He's crying. Tears are bursting out of his eyes in droves. His shoulders start to shake sporadically and violently, and although he doesn't really open his mouth, a guttural sound, coming straight from the depths of his throat booms outwards and slams against the walls. I've heard him speak from that place before, but usually my knees are the ones quivering, not my lips. *Don't cry, Ayo. Don't cry.*

Of all the constants in this world, my father being a rock is the most unmalleable. Except now, he isn't a rock. He isn't even a pebble. In fact, to call him dirt feels generous, because then he would be a force of nature, at the very least. Now, my father, who could put the fear of God into me with only a jaw twitch, is just an old man. The gray on his head and beard don't make him look rigid or wise; they make him look frail, like he might actually crumble if I breathe too hard. This man isn't my father. For a while, at least, I've killed him and put this imposter in his place. My anger instantly dies at the thought.

Momo doesn't seem to share my empathy. Instead, she relaunches her anger at my father.

"No!" she cries. "You don't get to play the victim! Not after what you just said, you piece of shit!"

"Momo!" Jireh admonishes, reminding me she's here. She pulls on her friend's arm while her brother just stands there, gaze fixed on the ceiling. He has the same look on his face from back in the parking lot. Except cold, dead fiberglass stands in place of the stars.

With a venom that frightens me, Momo pulls her arm away from Jireh and points her index finger at my dad. She opens her mouth to speak, but the rhythmic beeping that had been some kind of sick metronome stretches out into one long beep, and my heart crawls its way into my throat. Shit. This is it.

My friends and family rush over to my body as doctors scurry in like a flock of birds with scary-looking machinery. Frantically, I turn to God Two.

"Make me not feel this," I say.

He shakes his head, like I was giving him a choice.

My hands find themselves grabbing on to the deity, viciously clenching his shoulders. "Please, please, please, please, *please!* I don't like feeling like this! Make it stop!"

"It's important that you feel this part, Ayo. After this, we can take you somewhere much happier, if you want. But for now, you need to experience this. You need to see for yourself."

"See what? See my best friends and family bawling their eyes out because of my inability to look both ways?!"

"Yes."

"Why would I—"

The next thing I know, the doctors push everyone out, and everyone save for my dad and Joshua fight back, trying to explain why they need to make sure I'm okay. The others seem to hold on to a shred of hope, but I think my dad knows. He always knows. He's always known.

The gods and I walk through the door behind them. When we get to the waiting room, my family sits on one side of the hallway while my friends sit on the other. Momo's glaring daggers at my dad, but he doesn't seem to care.

The tension in the room is so viscous and so bitter that it almost makes me gag. As for my old man, he's simply looking at his feet. His eyes are dead, and the look my mother gives him is the one you have when a stranger comes up to you like you're old friends and you're trying to remember where you've seen them before.

Jonah's gaze is still fixed on the ceiling, but his expression has changed, like he's looking for something. Jireh rubs his shoulder, but he either doesn't notice or doesn't care. I assume it's somewhere in the middle.

Finally, when it starts to feel like I might drown, Momo speaks. "When he gets out of this, you owe him an apology," she says through clenched teeth.

My father finally acknowledges her existence. "Maybe. Maybe we all do. But I think he also owes us one as well."

"EXCUSE ME?!" Momo screams, standing up. "What the fuck is *wrong* with you? Your only child is in the ICU, and you're telling me he should apologize to you? YOU?!"

"You spent all that time with him, right? Surely you—"

"Yes, he was a bit airheaded, but this piece of shit ran him over!" She's jamming her finger in Joshua's face. "Where's your anger? Where's your... Oh. Oh, I get it. You never loved him, did you?"

For a moment, my father comes back to life. His jaw twitches, and his eyes focus into a glare. "Don't talk about things you don't understa—"

"Ayo told me! You used to hit him! Both of you used to hit him when he pissed you off and you would call it discipline," she spat.

"It *was* discipline. Ayo struggled with following instructions, thus he led a life of... of aimlessness..." The new version of my dad returns, his eyes glazing over as he casts his gaze downward.

"Don't talk about him like he's already dead, you wretched, horrible... aaarrrrghhh!" She started out quietly, but progressively got louder and louder until she was screaming, so angry and bitter that she tumbled out of the English language.

"Shut up!" my mother seethed, standing up as well. "I've let you go this far because you're emotional, but that is my husband! Watch your mouth when you're talking to your elders."

"No! That's the problem. Respect this, respect that! Ayo told me if he so much as looked at you wrong, you'd pull his fucking ear. Well, guess what?" Jireh is ferociously pulling on Momo's arm, but Momo ferociously wrestles it away. "You can't hit him now, can you? You—"

"Momo, stop!" Jireh says, with more force than I think she's ever used in her life. "You're being unreasonable. Ayo already explained that—"

"I know what he said, but it's that toxic culture bullshit that killed him!" she screams, hysterical.

This isn't Momo. I must've killed her too, and I think that hurts more than my dad's indifference. Why the hell am I so fucking stupid?

"You people are—"

"I thought you asked him to stop talking as if Ayo's already dead," Jonah deadpans, still staring at the ceiling. "Calm down. You know how Ayo was about outbursts. Respect his memory at least."

"N-no! He's not dead. I'll apologize when he wakes up... I'll apologize when he..."

Jonah finally turns to her. "Sit down, Momo. You've said enough." He returns to staring at the fiberglass, and I immediately know I've twisted something in him as well. Something that I fear can't be untwisted.

Momo obeys and turns to Jireh. She stares at her friend for a few moments before leaning over and bitterly sobbing into her hair. Just like my mother, Jireh now has to be the pillar. The blood on my hands seems unwilling to ever dry.

The doctor walks in with a solemn look on her face. She doesn't need to say what she says next; her eyebrows and the way she sucks in her lips say more than enough.

"I'm incredibly sorry," she says, placing her hand on my dad's shoulder. "We tried everything we could, but—"

Louder. Louder than I've ever heard her, loud enough for the entire hospital and the entire world and the entire universe, loud enough for everywhere from the sun to all of Jonah's stars to hear her, Momo Sayuri screams from the bottom of her gut, and it's like a siren. The kind that digs into your bones, rattling your brain as it slams into your skull and into your chest cavity, just slightly out of sync with the beating of your heart. It's asking me why I couldn't just look to my left like everyone else. Why I always end up in situations that push me deeper and deeper into my own hands. Why I always let my grip tighten and tighten until there are marks on my thigh and I'm telling my girlfriend about it so she can use pleasure as a tarp so we don't have to see how much I'm bleeding.

Fuck. I want to puke again.

Stories

Two nights after Jonah signed his book deal, we walked all over his unnecessarily large neighborhood, just me and him, for hours on end, talking about whatever random bullshit that came to our heads. He had invited me, and I assumed Momo and Jireh would also be there, but to my surprise, it was just us.

"There's nothing wrong with being wrong, Jonah. Just admit it."

He cackled. "Admit what, Ayo? That you're dumb?"

"Ha, ha, very funny."

He punched my shoulder as we readied to cross the street. "What's funny is that you apparently need hearing aids."

"Well, I disagree. I'm telling you, man, it's 'he banished.'"

"Why would it be 'he banished'? He banished what?" He grabbed my shoulders and shook me back and forth. "What did he banish, Ayo?"

"Gah!" I exclaimed between giggles. "I don't know. Ask the writers, not me!"

"Yeah, well, they're writers. I think they know how English works, dumbass."

"Whatever." I blew him a raspberry as we crossed the street. I wasn't sure when exactly his expression shifted, but it wasn't long before I could hear it in his voice.

"Hey... You love Momo, right? Like, really love her?"

"Y-yeah." I stumbled, somehow still in the phase of my life where that word made me cringe.

He nodded but said nothing in return, and we kept walking silently for a moment or two. Then, in the middle of the street, Jonah just stopped and looked around. Without warning, he lowered himself and laid down flat on his back.

"Come lay with me, Ayo," he said, a hint of a smile in his voice as he tapped the asphalt next to him.

"Uh... I'm not sure if you know this, but—"

"Shhh," he said, placing his index against his lips. "The asphalt is nice. Come."

With a sigh, I crouched down and laid next to him. Unsure where to keep my hands, it surprised, but relieved me when his fingers interlocked with mine.

"I'm a taken man, Jonah," I joked.

"Oh, shut up. I just don't want you dipping," he said, still looking up at the sky.

"Why would I dip?"

"We're lying flat on our backs in the middle of the street. The average truck might not even see us."

"Oof. We should probably get up, then."

A soft breeze passed, accompanied by a minute of silence.

"Ayo?"

"Yeah?"

"What if I just stayed here?"

"Huh?"

"Like, what if I never get up and just stay here forever?"

"You can't, though."

Then he turned to me. "Why not? It's nice here, isn't it?"

Still holding his hand, I rise into a crouch.

"Super nice. If I was blind, I'd've thought it was memory foam."

"So why can't I stay here? What's wrong with me if I just stay here?" His voice trembled.

"Because then I'd spend the rest of my life believing that Katara said 'he banished.'"

Jonah didn't laugh, but he did that thing where air audibly comes out of your nose.

"My grandma died yesterday," he whispered.

I remember inwardly cursing because the only thing I'm worse at handling than sad people are *really* sad people.

"I-I'm really sorry to hear that. I'm sure she was a wonderful person. She'll be missed." By then, I was hurling insult upon insult at myself, because the voice that was saying those things didn't sound like mine, and what the voice was saying was some textbook bullshit.

"No, to both of those things," Jonah said, looking back up at the sky. "She was unbearably unpleasant. Even my mother is silently glad she's gone. She hated everyone but me. Said my writing reminded her of her husband."

"Oh."

"I just wanted her to read a book with my name on the cover... just one fucking book. You know how she went? Heart attack. They found her body crawling towards her Torah."

"Holy shit."

Finally, he turned to me and smiled jadedly. "Such is life, right?"

"W-well, I'm really sorry. I wish she got to leave on happier terms."

He sighed. "There are too many stories being told for all of them to have happy endings, Ayo. Her sister is probably over the moon right now."

"Such is life," was all my dumb ass could say.

"Such is."

I laid back down and Jonah turned on his side to face me. I followed suit.

"Can I lie here forever?" he said, squeezing my hand.

"Can I lie here with you?"

"You can't say that after you've already laid down, jackass."

I stuck my tongue out at him, and fast as a snake, he pinched it between his index finger and thumb.

"But yeah," he whispered, "I imagine it'd be marginally less boring if you stayed."

And so we laid there forever.

* * *

As Jonah and my family enter the hospital room, and as my killer sits outside, pulling his hair out, Jonah drops his gaze from the ceiling. Just like that night, the look on his face can only be described as one of exhaustion. Like he can't be bothered to look for what he knows he'll never find. And while everyone mourns in whatever way they know how, Jonah extends his tongue and pinches it between his index finger and thumb, all while a stubborn tear slides its way down his cheek.

It hurts, but I can't look away.

That is until Momo. Shocking me out of my Jonah-filled reverie, I turn and see her gripping my body's hand, loudly wailing, not caring who could hear her. Of course, I'm used to Loud Momo, just not necessarily Loud, *sad* Momo.

To everyone's surprise, the hand that lands on her shoulder is my dad's. She looks up at him with a jerk, and for a moment, I half expect her to slap him. Instead, her look of astonishment crumbles and a heavy sob charges through her body. She embraces my father, hugging him tighter than she ever hugged me.

"I'm so sorry," she says, her voice stuttering with the "hic" of each sob. My dad awkwardly places his hand on her head and soothingly rubs it. If I wasn't incredibly dead, I'd be smiling at the sight. My father isn't one for empathy, so it's heartwarming to know that he has it in him.

Mom pats Momo's back as Jireh grabs her hand. They almost look like an actual family—all except Jonah, who lets go of his tongue, turns, and places his forehead on the wall, presumably so no one can see him as his floodgates give way to his waterfalls. We can hear him, though. And perhaps that burns even more.

I walk up to Jonah and reach out my hand, knowing I'll phase right through him. Before we come into contact, however, I hear a snapping sound and my vision switches from a fully furnished room to a white... everywhere.

The shift in my surroundings is too sudden, and again, I lose my balance and find myself on my ass. What my ass is on, I'll just have to accept that I'll never know.

"Wait," I say, scrambling to my feet, turning back to see God One and God Two. "Why'd you do that?"

"I think you've seen enough," God Two says, "Any more and you'd probably never get to enjoy your afterlife."

"No... No, no, no, no, no! You *have* to take me back," I plead, spittle flying out of my mouth. "You have to take me back. You have to let me help them."

"Help them? Help them how? You're dead," God One scoffs.

"I don't know! Can't you guys do something? You're literally gods, what the fuck are you useful for if you can't even—"

"Hey! Watch it." God One's eyes narrow, but I can't find it in myself to care.

"Watch what? What're you gonna do, kill me? How about you fucking take—"

"Stop." God Two says. His voice is level, so much so that it's far more frightening than God One's growl.

I stop.

"Listen," he says, "I know it's incredibly difficult. But you have to understand that you're not the only human on Earth, or even the only human who died at 11:12pm on the third Saturday in May. This world is a perpetual motion machine, and it has to take on and lose weights to stay in motion. I'm sorry, but I really hope you can understand."

I can't *fucking* understand. None of this makes sense. None! I got pancaked by a truck and instead of being a splatter on the pavement, I'm somehow alive and watching the people I love cry over a dead version of me! Yet, this immortal being is asking me to "understand"?

I open my mouth to cuss him out, but at the last second, I bite my tongue and shut my eyes. *Breathe, Ayo. Breathe.* If I yell, I'll cry, and if I cry, I'll get nowhere. I have no reason not to believe God Two, so if what he's saying is true, then I have all of time in my hands, in theory... Just never enough to actually fix what I've broken.

But then I remember who I'm talking about, and my chest sags in relief. These are my friends and family—Momo, Jireh, and Jonah have each other and their individual gifts to propel them forward, and my parents went from trekking several miles to school everyday in pairs of broken sandals to living in the suburbs of the land of opportunity. They're gonna be fine. They're gonna be fine, because they don't need me. They never have. And now I have all the time in the world to see it for myself.

I take a shaky breath and fold my arms. "So now what?"

"Now," God Two says, back to his cheery self, "you can go wherever, whenever you want! Perhaps you'd like to watch the original *Romeo And Juliet*? Or perhaps you have more violent tastes and would like to watch Hulk Hogan beat Andre the Giant?

Humans say this a lot, but the world is truly at your fingertips! Ayo, you can—"

"Do aliens exist?"

"Pardon?"

"I mean, God One said you guys' bodies adjust to our culture, so I'm just wondering if you also adjust to our species. 'Cause that would mean that humans were self-centered when we imagined God looking like us, and that in turn would mean—"

"I feel like that isn't particularly relevant right now."

"Right. Right, sorry. What were you saying?"

"That you can spectate anyone at any time."

"For how long?"

"Until it's time to sleep."

That stops me in my tracks. "Sleep? What does that mean?"

Obviously, I have an inkling, but I ask anyway. Just the mention of a death after dying feels like it'll—

"It means poof," God One explains. "Nothing."

"Do I get to choose when that happens?"

"Yep," God Two says.

"Or *if* that happens?"

"Correct."

My shoulders relax. Why anyone in their right mind would choose to die after dying is beyond me. Thankfully, I've been given a choice. I've been given a *choice*.

"Alright, man-tits," God One says, stuffing his hands into his pockets. "When and where do you want to go first?"

God Two pipes up. "I recommend the year 3073. Humans successfully manage to digitally simulate the creation of the multiverse and…"

His excited ramblings fade into the background because my mind begins running through all my options. I then *lose* said mind when I realize there's no end in sight. I can see it all. I can literally see it all! Every thing at every time that I want! Everything from the first fly to land on a pile of shit to the last human to tread the Earth. The concept of future, past, and present is pretty much useless because they're all accessible to me at a moment's notice! "Waiting" and "patience" are essentially just empty words at this point! Is this what gods feel like? Am I a god? Holy shit! What if I'm a god? Not to jump the gun here, but if I'm a god, does being a Christian technically make me Jesus? Holy shit... I'm Black Jesus! Does that mean I'm—

Momo. Momo, Jonah, Jireh, and all the little pieces of them that I took with me halt me in my tracks.

"...and basically, humans are able to live for many centuries after the sun absorbs the earth because you guys make these little space colonies in ships that travel for thousands of years at a time. It's a little sad that some people live and die without ever seeing the outside of a ship, but most of the vessels are about a quarter the size of the moon, so there's a lot to see—"

"I know."

God Two stops. "What was that?"

"I know where I want to go."

"Oh, was I that convincing?" he asks, visibly proud of himself.

God One's eyes lock with mine, and after a flicker of a moment, he nods at me. I don't know how, but I know he's thinking what I'm thinking, and I know he's on board.

"Sure," we say, and God Two looks at the two of us, wondering what the hell he missed.

Part 2

For All My Runaway Hertz

BEING

"You know, one time," Jireh once said to me, "Jonah told me that if there was a God, and he is all good, and if we're all in his image, then he's been slacking for the past two hundred thousand years."

This was back in like, sophomore year, I think? I remember Jonah had been out of town for a book signing for one of his favorite authors, and Momo had a sleepover thing with the other theater kids. Jireh invited me over that night, and because I was bored as hell, I agreed. We ended up having a really good time, and decided we would spend more time with just the two of us, a promise we struggled to keep once the status quo returned.

"Really? Sounds like the kind of shit he'd spontaneously say out of nowhere, to be fair." I hit her with a twelve-hit combo and the smuggest smirk I could muster.

We were sitting crisscross-applesauce in her room, our burning eyes only a foot away from the television. Her PS4 producing the sounds of a small hurricane acted as background music to our battle.

"You ass!" she squealed, then kicked my arm, causing me to miss an ultimate jutsu.

With a massive grin, she caught me in a combo and seeing as I had no substitutions left, I was forced to just sit there and get my ass whooped.

"Ha! Catch this L real quick!" she proclaimed, as my health bar seemed to whimper and shrink at the might of her onslaught.

Eventually, it was entirely depleted and she shot up and did a little dance.

Now, I couldn't just stand there and let her make me her bitch, so I picked up one of her cookies and dropped it in her orange juice.

"Hey!" she gasped. "What the hell was that for?" With a roar, she climbed over me and trapped me in a choke hold. Heh, I remember inwardly pleading with myself not to pop a boner. *Titties don't exist. Titties don't exist. Titties don't exist.*

Eventually, she released me and picked up one of her cookies before placing it in my apple juice.

"Bitch!"

"Hehe."

"I'll kill you!"

"You literally did it to me two seconds ago!"

"That was orange juice!"

"So?"

"Don't compare tarnishing copper to tarnishing gold!"

Jireh rolled her eyes. "Drama queen."

With a sigh, I placed the cup against my lips and took a sip. "Nope. Still fantastic. Not even you can ruin apple juice."

As I was sipping my life force, Jireh pressed her toe against the foot of my cup, causing my drink to spill all over me. I sputtered, then shrugged, pulling my shirt up to my tongue.

"Ewww!" Jireh whined as I licked apple juice off of Gumball's face. I must have been about two or three licks in when she hesitantly sighed.

"Ayo?"

"Yeah?"

"Momo told me... about the marks."

"Oh."

"I'm sorry."

"It's fine, don't apologize."
"Do you want to talk about it?"
I didn't say anything.
"I'm sorry."
"It was stupid, I guess."
"No—"
"I'm—"
"I'm not sure what it was. Maybe I was crazy or whatever, but I went from sad to angry real fast, and well, that... happened. It happened."
"Why were you angry?"
My only response was more silence.
"I'm sorry."
"Sometimes, Jireh, I feel... small."
"Small?"
"Like a Lego character among humans. Like I could get stepped on and be nothing more than an 'ouch.' I didn't like that, and this... happened."

"It happened," was all she had said in return.

I was about to go back to licking Gumball when Jireh laid back and rested her head on my leg.

"I think I understand what you're saying. I guess I see it more like I'm a cardboard cutout. Like everyone's talking at me, but no one's talking *to* me. Like I could tip over if I so much as touched anyone."

I remember having to remind myself to close my mouth. Jireh? Jireh Eddison? Jireh, who entered parties riding on Momo's back and had the balls to dip chocolate chip cookies in apple juice? That Jireh? By no means was she the loudest of us, but I didn't think there was a single person in the world who didn't genuinely like her. If Momo was the sun and Jonah was the moon, then Jireh and her laughter were like a cool breeze on a warm summer day.

"I would pick you up," I told her.

"Huh?"

"If you tipped over, we would pick you up."

"I'm pretty sure you're supposed to help me tear down the cutout."

I shrugged. "That's all I've got for you."

Jireh chuckled. "You've stopped, right?"

"Yeah."

"Yeah?"

"Yeah. It almost feels stupid now, because I know people go through real shit. People lose people they love. People have actual disorders that affect the way they live. I'm just stupid and bitching over nothing. Even so, sometimes, it gets… bad."

"What makes it get bad?"

I took a moment to gather my thoughts.

"I'm sorry."

"Jireh, you don't have to apologize every time I hesitate."

"Heh, my bad."

"You're fine. I guess it can be anything, something as small as telling a bad joke, or failing a test, or I suppose sometimes it just feels easier to let it be bad. Either way, I sort of, enter myself? I think? The point is, it's just me and my mind, and it never takes me to good places."

"Do you ever feel small with us?"

"No—"

She grips my ankle.

"Yeah. All the time."

"Ayo, why the hell do you still hang out with us, then?"

I paused. My next words were deeply calculated, but I still cringed into myself with every syllable.

"Because then we'd drink beer and try to fit Jonah into a garbage can. Or we'd try riding our bikes off ramps like sixth graders and twist our ankles. Or maybe a certain redhead will try and tarnish my liquid gold—"

"That's oil."

"And when that happens, I don't feel small. I feel like the world is an elaborate Lego structure and I get to stomp as hard and as much as I want on those small bits and pieces. I love that. I *love* that. I want it over and over again." I looked down at her and poked my finger on her nose. "And I only get it with you guys."

Jireh wiggles and pushes my hand away. "And what happens when... if you get angry again?"

"Then Momo'll push my fat ass deeper into therapy and stuff more of those stupid pills down my throat. Or something. I'm happy right now, and that's gotta be enough for now."

"Do you think the therapy and stupid pills help?"

"Hmm. I think the therapy and stupid pills do help, in a way. I just find them to be a little overkill sometimes. Most times. Don't tell Momo I said that. She likes the therapy and stupid pills."

Jireh gave me a worried look.

I bit my lip. "Please?"

"You know, Ayo, we don't say this enough, and I'm glad Jonah isn't here so I can speak for him, but we're all glad we met you. It's really easy being your friend."

"Thanks. That means a lot."

"How badly are you cringing right now?"

"I've passed the quota for the amount of emotion a Nigerian can show. I am now deceased."

"Nice. Wanna get back to the game?"

"Thought you'd never ask."

So she reached over my bonerless pants and grabbed her controller while I placed Gumball's face in my mouth and sucked out as much apple juice as I could.

We went back into the game, and I took and distributed many more Ls that night.

* * *

Can you believe it?!" Momo yelled in Past-me's ear as she did unspeakable things to Past-me's hair. "OUR FINAL YEAR!"

"I know, right? I'm so excited!" Jireh added, shaking her brother back and forth. The brother in question continued reading his manga like she wasn't there, but Jireh was far too excited to notice the subtle insult like Past-me did.

"What about you, Ayo? You don't look so hyped," Jonah remarked, still not looking up from his book.

"Uh, yeah, of course I am. Can't wait to get out of this hellhole…" Past-me's voice cracked.

"Right?" Momo agreed. In her excitement, she pulled on Past-me's hair so hard that I'm sure he lost consciousness for a while. He didn't complain though. It was Momo; she could pull any part of him as hard as she wanted.

It's certainly an unsettling sensation, watching myself talk to my friends. Especially when you know that these are very real iterations of us. There is no main timeline. This Ayo, this Momo, this Jireh, and this Jonah are as real as the corpse lying in the hospital bed nine months from now. And that makes my brain backflip in sync with my stomach. It's one thing to reminisce about my past, but it's another thing entirely to see it with my own eyes. God Two places his hand on my shoulder, I think, but I'm too engrossed to really care. It feels so real, and it only gets worse every time I remember that it is.

"Momo, need I remind you that Ayo's hair is much closer to his scalp? He doesn't have the luxury of getting his hair mauled by you the way I do," Jonah said.

Past-me popped his lips. "I'm ninety-nine percent sure there's something racist about what you just said, but I can't put my finger on it, so I'll let it slide."

"Mhm…" he droned as he flipped a page.

Jireh thumped his head. No response.

"I agree with Ayo," Momo said, pulling Past-me's hair as if inflicting pain on him helped prove her point. "Besides, it isn't mauling. I'm going to make his hair even more beautiful. His people call it *plating*."

That was false. The abomination Momo Sayuri was doing to Past-me's hair was nothing less than a travesty, but she's the most gorgeous creature in existence and Past-me—and Present-me—had no self-esteem, so he emphatically nodded. "You're gonna be so jealous of my magnificent mane, Jonah," he said.

This time, Jonah did look up at him, and his smile made Past-me smile. But then he went back to reading and Past-me was left smiling to himself like an idiot. As quickly as he could without looking offended, he dropped his smile and acted natural. Which was difficult to do when there's an angel sent from the heavens molesting your hair with a radiant smile on her face.

As if seeing him isn't crazy enough, I can almost read Past-me's mind. I only have a vague memory of the thoughts that went through my head back then, but the aura of thought and feeling is nevertheless nostalgic, and though I'm not of their world anymore, the memory of how Momo smelled that night feels so vivid that a small, subconscious part of me wonders if I'm alive again.

"Hey Ayo," Momo said, pulling on Past-me's hair even more. "Favorite hentai tag?"

"Loli," Past-me said immediately. I mouth the words with him.

"Pedo," Momo shot back.

"Um, we prefer the term 'lolicon,'" Jonah said, still not looking up from his book. "Get it right."

Jireh clicked her tongue. "Well, *we* prefer the term 'pedo.'"

Momo, Jireh, and Past-me laughed, and again, Jonah looked up at Past-me with a grin before going back to his book. Then something small, but significant shifts. Perhaps it's the nostalgia, perhaps it's a higher power, but I feel the grin. Somewhere in my gut, or in my chest, it resonates. Because for some reason, his smile draws me back to the man we saw all those months ago. I know what they said, and I know they haven't forgotten yet, but I feel like they wanted to. Like if they could, they would wipe the image from their minds. It stings, but I suppose it makes sense. If I wasn't in my circumstances, I'd probably hope to never think about him again, too. Still, my chest pangs with contrasting emotions at the knowledge that they'll eventually forget me as well.

God Two seems to read my mind. "Most people relive their memories over and over again for a reason. Usually it's something more triumphant, but I imagine this holds great significance to you. Enjoy it, Ayo. It will quite literally last forever."

I take a deep breath.

"Jonah, shouldn't you be at your computer? When's your next deadline?" Jireh asked, karate chopping his head.

In true Jonah fashion, he didn't look up from his book. "Tomorrow, I think."

"Tomorrow?!" Momo and Jireh simultaneously yelled. Past-me yelled as well, but to no one's surprise he was a couple beats behind.

Jonah looked up from a full panel of Noelle-tits to meet Jireh's gaze. "Hey, have you sent in your application yet?"

"Don't change the subject!" she said, slapping his head. "Also, yes. Unlike you, I actually give a shit."

"I like how you just didn't answer the question," Momo said, and committed further war crimes to Past-Me's hair for good measure.

"What question?" Jonah deadpanned.

Past-me winced at Momo's onslaught. "Smooth," he said.

Jonah flicked his fingers at him.

"By the way, Ayo," Jireh said.

Past-me gulped. He knew where this was going. He wished and wished and wished he was wrong, but the universe had a way of telling him to suck its dick. I should know. He's me now. And I'm kinda dead.

"Have you figured out what club you wanna join yet?" Jireh asked.

Past-me looked like he wanted to puke. They were asking questions; big questions that would shape their futures. They had deadlines and places to go. Meanwhile, he was still stuck on which club he wanted to join, and not for the first time, he felt like an ant trapped in a snow globe.

"Uh... nope. Not yet," Past-me replied, desperately hoping they didn't hear the crack in his voice. He hated his voice. I hate his voice.

"You should come back to the poetry club," Jonah said, and Past-me looked like he practically shat out his heart.

"You were in the poetry club?!" Momo and Jireh hollered, though Momo's bellow was significantly more bone-rattling.

"Oh yeah... that was supposed to be a secret, wasn't it?" Jonah said absentmindedly. The assbag was still reading his fucking book.

"Uh... yeah. I-I joined for a few weeks last year, but it wasn't a big deal. I just left, 'cuz it wasn't that big a deal so don't worry about it," Past-me said. I never realized it, but evidently my accent would come out whenever I got nervous. Wonder why they never pointed it out.

"Wait, is that where you two kept vanishing off to last year?" Jireh asked.

Momo twisted Past-me's hair. "I kind of just assumed they were fucking."

Jireh's eyebrows spiked as she grinned. "Me too!"

They high-fived.

In full, voice-cracking glory, Past-me piped up. "N-no, we weren't! It was just something dumb I tried."

Jonah read in silence for a while. Then, still looking down at his book, he pulled at a loose thread on his duvet. "He was really good, though. Everyone thought he'd been writing his whole life."

"Okay, I see you, Ayo." Momo mercilessly pulled on Past-me's hair as a reward while Jireh clapped.

"But then he fucking dipped," Jonah said, releasing the thread and murdering whatever buzz could have possibly formed. In secret, Jireh hit his back with her heel, but Past-me saw. Past-me always saw.

"I guess I just didn't think I was as good as everyone else thought I was," Past-me said, grateful for Momo's onslaught making him wince instead of whatever stupid expression he would've been wearing otherwise.

Now, what I said is partly false. I know for a *fact* that I wasn't nearly as good as Jonah painted me to be. I got a lot of claps for my poem, but I could ultimately tell I made it awkward. Everyone else talked about real issues. Their parents splitting, loved ones dying of both pronounceable and unpronounceable illnesses. One girl even wrote the most beautiful poem that paralleled the life cycle of a rose to the time she tried to take her own life because people refused to see past her appearance. Everyone's art came from a place that was true to themselves at their core.

Me? My poem was about how I didn't like how Zoloft made me feel. That was it. A few metaphors for being sleepy, a line I stole from a Tumblr comment section, and bam—a completely underwhelming, yet self-indulgent attempt at poetry. I saw it in their expressions, in the way they clapped or, for some, snapped their fingers. I didn't belong there. I was too whole, and that only made me feel more incomplete.

Past-me must have been going through the same thought channel that I was, because he scrambled to redirect the current. "Well, Momo's got some great news, guys."

Momo froze. And while I know Past-me genuinely felt bad for breaching her trust, a part of him was a bit relieved that the barrage on his scalp had ceased.

"Oooooo," Jireh said, eyebrows dancing. "And just what is this good news that I haven't heard?"

"W-well, it's nothing. I don't even know why Ayo brought it up. Forget about it. Back to Ayo—tell us more about these poems you've written," she said, going back to twisting my hair, albeit with a lot less vigor.

I remember my exact thought process here. Or at least, I remember that I had none. Just the idea of the conversation flowing back to me and my purposelessness made my heart race. So much so that I did something unimaginably stupid. I pushed.

"Oh, come on, Momo. Tell them," Past-me said.

"No. We agreed we'd keep it on the down-low."

The hurt in her voice was evident, and it made the air heavier. The only problem was that if Past-me stopped, he'd have to face that awkwardness, and the disapproving gaze of the Eddison twins, and just thinking about that took the air out of his lungs. So he kept going, pretending he couldn't read the social cue. Pretending he wasn't a piece of shit. Like he isn't a piece of shit.

"Oh, come on," he said. "It's a big deal."

"Ayo, really I—"

"Guys, Momo got accepted into the American Academy of Dramatic Arts!" No one said anything. "Come on. It's the AADA. This is great news!" Past me said.

Jonah looked up from his book, and bit the inside of his cheek as his gaze bounced from mine to Momo's.

After a few moments of silence. Momo finally spoke, still slowly plating my hair. "We agreed we'd keep that a secret."

Past-me knew what he'd done. He one hundred percent understood the gravity of his actions, but he was too far in. He could either apologize and face even more awkwardness, or he could be a coward and play dumb.

"Well yeah, but these are our homies. We tell them everything," Past-me said.

Momo let go of his hair. "It doesn't matter." There was a soft hardness behind every word. If they had sound effects, each of them would slowly float to the ground but still land with a *thud*. "You promised. You promised you would keep it a secret."

"Momo, it's not that big a deal, this is something incredible you've done. What reason could you possibly have for keeping it a secret? This is something we should celebrate together. It's something important."

"I know what you're doing, Ayo." Her voice was still hard, but now it was also trembling, like there were chains locked around her words moments from breaking. "And it's wrong. You can't break promises when you see fit just because you want to change the subject. This is so unlike you. You're being selfish."

"Okay, Momo. I think maybe you're being a tad bit overdrama—"

Momo didn't let Past-me finish. She slammed her palms against his back, got up from Jonah's bed, and stormed out of the room.

The awkwardness that Past-me feared came in full force and the air in the room got so heavy that it hurt to breathe, despite me not breathing the same air as them. I think.

"Holy shit. I didn't think it was that big a deal, ya know?" I said after a good thirty seconds of agonizing silence.

"When we were in sixth grade," Jireh said, playing with the same loose thread Jonah had toyed with earlier. "Momo scored the leading role in a huge play at the end of the year. She was stoked to go, and marked her calendar, but then she realized the play was on Jonah and I's birthday celebration. We had agreed to do a sleepover and had already planned out all these fun things, so Momo dropped out. Immediately. She'd been praying and praying and praying for months that she'd get that role, but once she realized that it would make her have to backtrack on our promise, she canceled it without a second thought. Because she's crazy like that. And believe me, I knew what she was pushing aside for me, and I could've easily moved the sleepover date, but I didn't. Momo loves assholes. It's what she does. The least we can do is try to not be assholes. Maybe that doesn't make any sense and I'm just going on random bullshit tangents that don't really say anything, but—"

"The last bathroom on the right," Jonah said, still reading. "That's where she goes when she's upset. Squeezes her six-foot-three ass into the bathtub and stares at her feet for an hour or two."

"Yeah," Jireh added, "she's crazy like that."

Past-me softly nodded and got up from the bed. With feet made of lead, he trudged out of the room and into the hallway. The gods and I follow him, and the whole time I'm looking at Past-me.

I resist the urge to spit.

When he reached the door, Past-me took a deep breath, one that lasted a bit too long. He was stalling. Sigh.

Finally, he knocked tentatively, like he thought the door would shatter upon impact.

"Go away," Momo said. Her voice was clogged and wet.

"You don't even know who it is yet."

"Are you Ayo?"

"Y-yeah."

"Then go away."

Past-me sighed and rested his forehead against the door.

"Listen, Momo," he said. "I'm sorry, okay? But you—"

"Just be honest!"

Silence stretched through the door and came between us.

"You're right. You're always right. I got scared and I panicked and I deserve for you to yell at me and destroy my hair and tell me to go away and—"

"I was making it more beautiful."

"What?"

"Your hair. You said I was making it more beautiful."

"Right. Right, of course. That's what I meant. Can I come in?"

She sniffled. "I'm still mad at you."

"I know, and I deserve that, and I don't deserve you, but I'm sorry. I'm really, really sorry, and I love you and I'm sorry."

No sound came through the bathroom door.

"I'm sorry."

She sniffled again. "Alright come in."

With the same timorousness he used to knock on the door, Past-me opened it and was met with Momo's glare. She clearly hadn't quite forgiven him yet.

Momo was tall, and this was made even more prominent when you saw her sitting in a relatively small bathtub, hugging her knees, and glowering at her boyfriend. She looked like what Goliath would look like if he thought he was David.

"I can't believe you did that," she said.

Past-me sighed and lowered his head as he walked over to the bathtub. "I know, and you're right. I'm selfish and I shouldn't have done that and I'm really, *really* sorry."

"Saying sorry doesn't make it okay, Ayo." Her lips quivered.

Past-me crouched by the bathtub and stretched out his hand. She was still glaring at him, but Momo didn't hesitate to take his hand. She never did.

"I'm a shitty boyfriend, no doubt about it. No amount of apologizing will change that. But I want you to know that I am genuinely sorry. And whatever I can do to make you forgive me, I'll do."

Momo sniffed and tightened her grip on Past-me's hand. "You aren't a shitty boyfriend."

"You're right." He nodded. "I'm a shitty person."

"No," she said with a small chuckle. "I just… I don't know. I could never not love you, but I want to punch you more than I want to hug you right now."

Past-me nodded again. "Honestly, I don't mind either." He smiled when Momo laughed.

"I'm sorry. Really sorry. But, if you don't mind me asking, why were you so against me telling them the good news? The AADA is a fantastic school, even if it sounds like the name of a company that sells lawsuits. Hold up, is it actually a fantastic school? Is that why you didn't want them to know? I'll be honest, I didn't actually check. I just assumed since it's in New York it must be a big deal. That's my bad. I should have looked it up—"

"I didn't get in."

Another awkward silence slumped between us.

"What?"

"The school. It's a good school, but I l-lied. I didn't get in."

"Why would you—nevermind. That's a stupid question."

"I'm sorry for lying to you. I was just so confident when I sent the application. When I got the email I wasn't even sad, just embarrassed."

"I get it. Believe me, I get it. But you know I would never think differently of you because of some letter, right?"

Honestly, as much as I want to throw him off a bridge, I'm genuinely proud of Past-me. I remember consoling Momo, but the entire ordeal was uncomfortable for me, and the day after I was completely emotionally drained from not only being vulnerable, but watching someone else be vulnerable. I coughed it up to not being in my comfort zone, but I never imagined this would be what it looked like from outside myself. While I was alive, I often had moments where it felt like I was watching myself from above, and every time, *every* time, I hated what I saw. I hated how I sounded, how I looked, and how other people reacted to me and every trail of dumbassery that I left in my wake. But now that I'm dead and completely separated from myself, I don't. I can actually, literally see myself from a third-person perspective, and I don't hate what I'm looking at. It's such an unfamiliar sensation that I'm not sure what the proper reaction is supposed to be. Despite the fact that I know that Past-me feels like shit right now, I chuckle. I chuckle because, although he can't tell, he's doing the right thing... ish. And that, though it's too late now, feels good. I can't help but want to reach out to him and ask him to chuckle as well.

"Of course I know that. I'm just stupid, I guess." Momo leaned down and rested her forehead on Past-me's. "You're stupid, too," she whispered.

He smiled. "Very."

Her fingers interlocked with Past-me, and she fiercely gripped them. "You know, you have nothing to be ashamed of."

"I do," he replied. "I have lots of things to be ashamed of."

"No."

"Yes."

"There's nothing wrong with not knowing what you want to do yet. Lots of people our age don't know."

He watched her eyes flutter closed, and followed suit. "That's true, but it doesn't help. Momo, I'm... bad."

"Bad how?"

"I don't know. Just bad, I guess."

"Stop hiding, Ayo. Speak." Her grip tightened once more.

"I'm being honest. I—"

"Ayo, speak. *Please.*"

"I feel like humans operate at a certain frequency. The way they speak, eat, joke, talk, walk, laugh, cry, and all the other shit that makes them tick. I think operating at that frequency is what separates us from monkeys or whatever."

"And?"

"And sometimes, when I'm watching you guys desecrate the name of tennis, or when I go to a concert, or see people running through the halls on the last day of school, I feel it. I *hear* it. Somewhere in my gut. So loud, so deep, so *angry* that it hurts."

Her voice fell to a whisper. "What does it say?"

Past-me bit his lip. "That I'm a few hertz shy."

Immediately after he said that, Momo wrapped her long arms around his neck and pulled his face up to hers. A kiss laced with all the words she couldn't say. It held the I'm-sorry-you-feel-this-way, and the I-forgive-you-for-being-an-asshole that I didn't deserve. It was just as much an explosion of love as it was a blow to the chest. Because as much as it swore to Past-me that he mattered, as much as it made him feel less like a deformed demon sent to torture itself and more like a living, breathing human being, it also reminded me that I'm not. And there aren't enough words to accurately describe how much that fucking sucks.

After what felt like an eternity of self-envy, Momo pulled away for a breath before placing her forehead against his once more. "You taste like jollaw rice," she whispered.

Past-me giggled. "It's *jollof* rice."

Momo's body shook with her laughter. "Oh my God."

"I can't believe you called it 'jollaw'!" Past-me laughed harder.

His laughter infected Momo, and her giggles stopped her from successfully biting Ayo's nose. "That's what I thought it was!"

When the two eventually calmed down, they closed their eyes again and subconsciously synced their breaths.

"Milf," Ayo said, eyes still closed.

After a breath, Momo's eyebrows furrowed. "You're gonna have to give me more than that. What?"

"My favorite hentai genre is milf."

"I like mindbreak."

"Holy shit. You're crazier than me."

"You bet. Hey…"

"What?"

"Two things."

"Hit me."

"One. I'll stuff my bra to look more Milf-like if you'll wear a choker with my name on it."

"Done."

"You just want to wear a choker with my name on it, don't you?"

"More than anything I've ever wanted in my entire life. Also, your tits are already amazing."

"Thanks. Two. How much you wanna bet Jonah and/or Jireh is behind that door right now?"

As if on cue, Jireh's hushed voice rang out from behind the door. "Stop poking me with your elbow! I'm trying to listen!"

"I just want to take a shit," Jonah complained, not even bothering to lower his voice.

"Come in, losers." Momo said.

Sheepishly, Jireh pushed the door open and grinned like she was caught stealing cookies.

"I'm sorry," she said, dragging out the "ee" sound.

Jonah shrugged and walked in like he owned the place. "I really just want to take a shit."

"There's a bathroom downstairs," Momo said, raising an eyebrow.

"This one's closer—" Jonah began, but Jireh couldn't wait.

She shook her head and leaped into the bathtub, ripping Momo away from me as her hands wrapped around the taller girl's neck.

"Momooooooo!" she cried. "You don't need to hide anything! You're special and great and perfect and—"

Momo patted her back. "Thanks, Jireh," she croaked. "But you're killing me."

Jireh pulled away and slammed her lips into Momo's cheek so hard that she winced. "I just want you to know that that university is going to cringe so hard when they look at what you accomplish and you're going to rub it in their stupid, stuck-up faces."

Momo laughed, her eyes moist. "That means a lot. I'm sorry I didn't tell you guys. What can I do to make it up to you?"

"What the hell are you talking about?" Jireh said, pinching Momo's cheek. "You don't owe us a single—"

"Chick-fil-A," Jonah stated.

Past-me nodded. "I concur."

They fist-bumped.

Rolling her eyes, Jireh turned back to Momo, then closed her eyes and took a deep breath. "I like ugly bastards."

Momo blinked.

"You guys were talking about hentai tags. Ugly bastard's my favorite."

"Oh, I get it," Momo finally said. "That's... that great, Jireh."

Her face crumpled. "Well don't say it like *thaaat*!"

"Say it like what?"

"Like *that*! Now I feel like a creep! What do you think, Ayo?"

Past-me blinked. "I mean it's certainly an acquired taste, I'm sure."

Jireh groaned as she leaned on the other side of the tub and stared at the ceiling. "I'm a freak."

"No you're not!" Momo said. "Jonah, help us out here."

Jonah lifted his gaze from the toilet and turned to his sister. "You disgust me."

"Oh yeah?" Jireh clapped back. "What's *your* favorite tag?"

He shrugged. "I mean I already said it was loli, didn't I?"

The whole group collectively groaned, and a smirk appeared on Jonah's face. It was so smug and so Jonah-like that it had me blinking away tears. I'll never get to make new memories with them. Never get to talk about hentai or video games or any of the other shit that we were way too passionate about. A whole new wave of regret hits me again. *Was it that hard, Ayo? To just look both ways?*

Regardless, now I'm torn. I want to watch them, for today, and for tomorrow and for forever until it ends with the truck, and then I want to start all over again from before I even met them. However, I know that now that I'm outside of the equation, now that I'm not texting Momo at midnight to help me with math homework, now that they can go back to dominating art competitions without looking for some way to include me, their potential is literally limitless. I want to see that. I want to see their names in lights and the Oscars and the sales numbers. I want to see the lives they save, and those who envy them. I want to see the little moments where they remember me and smile. I'm ravenous for it.

"I mean, I get that it's cute or whatever, but why the hell did you choose to come here first? Also, why're you kids so horny?" God One says from behind me.

With my first true grin in a while, I turn towards the gods. "So that I can be sure of where I want to go next." My grin widens, because grinning felt good back in that bathroom, and it sure as hell feels good now.

"You're horny so you can be sure of where you want to go next?" he asks.

"What?"

"You're the one who said it, man."

Sigh.

Told

It's difficult to determine whether or not Future-Jireh is a glow up from Past-Jireh. On one hand, she looks great. Her expression is firmer, her voice is harder, and she walks like that's what she was born to do, regardless of whether or not there are people in front of her. The happy-go-lucky girl who followed her brother around grew into a woman who could intimidate you into not saying "hi" simply by existing.

Except now, ten years later, she isn't a famous singer. Her name isn't in lights and her voice isn't on the radio. Jireh Eddison is an insurance agent. And not just any agent, either—she works for State Farm. Let that sink in.

Her usually curly ginger hair has been straightened and tied back into a ponytail, but that's not all that's changed. She's wearing a black, medium-length pencil skirt and a white blouse rolled up to her elbows. It was the kind of regulated, in-the-box attire that Jireh hated. It makes sense, though. She's an employee and she has rules to follow, something I think is currently on her mind as she's walking towards what I can only assume is her boss' office with an expression that doesn't match the hesitance in her step.

From an objective standpoint, though Jireh hasn't exactly fulfilled her dreams (yet), that doesn't necessarily mean she's unhappy. Maybe she loves doing insurance. Maybe she—

Jireh knocks on the door of a Mr. Clay and a voice way too high-pitched to belong to a Mr. Clay says, "Come in!"

She walks in, followed by me and the gods phasing through the wall like a bunch of sickass ninja ghosts.

Mr. Clay's office is spacious, much larger than the flyspeck cubicles Jireh and her co-workers have. The walls are adorned with various award plaques, so many that they don't even mean anything, and they outnumber the pictures of him and his family so much that those don't mean anything either. His desk is a beautiful mahogany structure with line patterns and his chair looks so leathery I fear it might crack just from me staring at it.

"Mrs. Eddison, mind taking a seat?" Mr. Clay squeaks.

"Thank you, sir," Jireh replies before sitting down. She almost sounds like a different person. Her voice came from a tight jaw, which it almost never did ten years ago, and now her eyes are anything but soft. It's oddly surreal. A few moments ago, I saw her leap into Momo's arms like a child and she sounded so much, for lack of a better word, younger. Now, I honestly wouldn't be surprised if God Two just made a mistake and finger-snapped us into the wrong person's future.

"Mind telling me what happened?" Mr. Clay asks, leaning back in his chair. The motion made his beer belly more pronounced, which in turn made his bald spot more pronounced, which in turn made the roughness of his pale skin more pronounced, and thus continued the trail of biases I was already forming against this man who's just living his life.

"It's Daniel, sir. He persistently makes inappropriate remarks and advances towards me." It's clear she's trying to keep it together. As much as she might be nervous for some reason, Jireh is angry. And I don't think I've ever said those words before. Not even as a joke.

"So let me see if I've got this straight. Your coworker is being inappropriate and you throw piping-hot coffee on him?" Mr. Clay leans forward and crosses his fingers, planting his elbows on his desk.

Jireh blinks. "Sir, he put his hand on me."

"So you gave him a third degree burn?"

"Sir! He placed his fucking hand on my a—" She stops and takes a breath before continuing. "Am I supposed to just sit there and smile like that's not fucking weird?"

He sighed. "You could've slapped his hand, could've cussed him out... Hell, you couldn've sprinkled his ass with holy water, but you didn't have to fucking baptize the guy. You know he could press charges if he wanted to? Half his face is redder than a baboon's ass!"

"You mean the piece of shit didn't deserve that? Are you fucking kidding me?!"

"Eddison, I know you're upset, but I'm still your boss. I'mma need you to watch your tone."

The woman wearing Jireh's body takes a deep breath. "I apologize, sir," she says through her teeth. "I'm just upset that the one groping women isn't in your office right now."

"Understandably so," Mr. Clay responds. "And believe me, he *will* face the proper consequences. Unfortunately, you left the interaction with a bad taste in your mouth while he left it as a bargain-bin Harvey Dent. Seems to me like he's more of the victim here, wouldn't you agree?"

Woman-in-Jireh's skin is speechless. "What? How on Earth could he—"

"You know what?" Mr. Clay says, leaning back into his chair again. "It's Friday. My kid's got a bullshit peewee soccer game that I gotta go to if I wanna sleep in my own bed tonight, and I'm sure your kids miss you more than I can imagine, so why don't you take the rest of the day off? We can finish this discussion on Monday."

Pseudo-Jireh blinks again. "Are you trying to get rid of me?"

"I'm trying to get rid of conflict." Again, he interlocks his fingers. "Fergusson's gonna be at his cubicle with an ice pack pressed against the side of his face, and if he sees you, there's gonna be conflict. Go rest, Mrs. Eddison. You work the hardest around here anyways."

"Will I at least get paid?"

"There's gotta be some form of punishment."

Her face turned sour. "I understand. Have a nice weekend, sir. My regards to your son's soccer game."

Rigid, yet brimming with anger, Imposter-Jireh stands up and walks towards the exit, her fists clenched so tightly that I'm worried she might bleed.

As she reaches the doorway, she stops momentarily and takes a breath. "Is this why you won't give me a raise?" she asks, not turning back to him.

Suddenly looking very tired, Mr. Clay deflates with a sigh. "No. You're hotheaded, but a hard worker. Unfortunately, things haven't lined up yet."

"What does that mean? I've got kids to feed, sir."

Silence.

"Go home, Jireh."

Next to me, God One puts his hands in his pockets. "Ten years is a real specific time frame, and why Jireh?"

I don't answer. Instead, I walk beside her as she trudges out of the office building and into the blistering Senoia heat. Her heels clack their way to a beat up Camry and she drops into it, her eye twitching.

She releases the biggest sigh I've ever heard before slamming her head against the steering wheel over and over again with so much venom that I fear I might see blood when she rears her head back. Thankfully, she slams her head on the wheel for seemingly the last time and it appears that was all the rage she had left because she just stays there, eyes closed and breath heavy. She does this for so long that I worry she might have fallen asleep.

I'm about to ask God Two if he can fast forward a few hours when Jireh pulls out her phone from her bag. It's a fairly conventional design, not too different from what we had when I was alive, just slimmer, with sharpened corners and nonexistent bezels. God, I sound like such an old—

"Hey, Jonah."

My heart freezes.

"Gah, nevermind." She presses a button on her phone and it turns off as she throws it into her bag. With more force than is perhaps necessary, Jireh twists her car key and backs out of the parking lot.

I turn to God Two. "Where's she going?"

"Walmart," he replies.

Jesus. Walmart? During the time I spent with her, Jireh's only options for grocery shopping were Publix, Target, or Death. No gray or in between for her. She almost flipped her lid when Momo and I took her to a Family Dollar.

"Can you take me to when she gets there?" I ask.

He nods and flicks his fingers.

My vision flashes to white before snapping into what I recognize as the produce section. A few meters ahead of me, Jireh picks up a pineapple and inspects it, looking very much like a mom. She *is* a mom, isn't she? That fully sinks in, and gets weirder and weirder the deeper it gets. I hope her romantic entanglements aren't limited to unprompted ass-grabbing.

With a nod, she places the fruit into her trolley—er... shopping cart, and wheels away.

Yes, I know it's disrespectful to think this way, but I can't help but find Jireh's current life rather boring. I mean, she didn't necessarily *have* to pursue music, but I always imagined she would lead a life of glamor. It just fit her personality. But if I had any doubts, the way she wiggles her hips to the generic pop music playing over the speakers makes me realize her life couldn't be any further from glamorous, and that leaves me terribly conflicted.

"How do you think you'd fit into her life if you were still alive?" God Two asks.

I turn to him. "What do you mean?"

"Well, it's obvious you were expecting more, right? How would you interact with her if you were still here?" His head is oddly tilted to the side.

I can't articulate why, but my heart and throat sink and I have to blink away tears. "That's a pointless question," I reply. "Me surviving wouldn't have changed anything."

Something weird happens to God One's eyebrows. "That's not what he asked, dumbass." He continues, but by then I'm not listening. I'm following Jireh out of the store and to her car.

After she puts, or rather throws her goods into the trunk and trudges around to the front seat, she sits down and once again places her head on the steering wheel, still humming that awful song from the store.

After staying in that position for at least a minute, she lets out a huge sigh and pulls her phone out from her bag. Then she taps a few times before placing it to her ear.

"Hey, Jonah..."

My heart freezes again.

"I-I don't know why I fight it all the time, I guess I... Nevermind. Call me. Call me. Call me. Call me. Call me... please. Please, call me, Jonah. I..." She whispers this last part, so far deep under her breath that I can't say for certain I'm not imagining it. "I can't... I can't breathe."

Then, she slams her fist against her steering wheel causing me to jump. She does it again and again, but it doesn't seem to make her feel better. In fact, every hit seems to enrage her further until she remembers her voice message is still going on. Her eyes widen and she clears her throat.

"Uh... yeah. That's gonna be it for today. I hope you're doing okay. How many 'call me's was that? Ah, it should be more than five, hopefully. I guess I'll go now, and um... I'm scared to go home early in a way, heh. I'm scared of my own children. I feel so stupid saying that out loud. I'm sorry for dragging this call on. Goodbye, Jonah." She pulls her phone away from her ear and tosses it into the cup holder beside her. Her car chokes to life and she drives out of the parking lot. On her way out, she drives over something, probably a speed bump, but my stupid brain can't help but imagine it's the Jireh I once knew.

For

Jireh's house is another thing about her that takes me by surprise. For starters, it isn't a house, it's an apartment. Which is fine on its own—Momo lived in an apartment, after all. The first issue is that the walls have stains poorly covered by plastic plants and the carpet smells like cat pee. The other issue is that my bedroom had more room than Jireh's living room. I don't know what I was expecting from someone living on an insurance agent salary, but to me it almost felt like this apartment was more of an antithesis to past-Jireh than future-Jireh was. Like all the light and joy that I'd come to associate with her had been sucked out by this place. I couldn't see it when she was getting groped by her coworker or ghosted by her twin, but this apartment tells me everything I wouldn't tell myself: Jireh is unhappy.

She stumbles into her apartment and locks the door without turning to look at it. Just as she manages to kick off her heels, two miniature Jirehs run out from nowhere and leap into her arms. It happens so fast that I almost jump. What's so freaky about seeing two fun-sized human beings who look just like my friend is something I'm unable to pinpoint, but I take several gulps nonetheless. Holy shit.

God Two turns to God One. "They're precious, aren't they?" He then clasps his fingers together.

God One shrugs. "One of them's got a big nose, and I'm pretty sure the girl's gonna have asymmetrical boobs when she's older."

God One and I turn and give him a questionable look of disgust. The edgy deity is oblivious. "What? You got a problem with mismatched breasts?"

"No, that's just not something you—" God Two is interrupted by one of the Mini-Jireh's ear-piercing laughter as her standard-sized version tickles her.

The other Mini-Jireh—I'll call him Mini-Jireh Two, since he's smaller—climbs up his mother's leg like a redheaded monkey, pulling on her clothes till he reaches her back. For a moment, he loses his balance, but pulls on his standard-sized version's hair to regain his balance. Standard-sized Jireh doesn't even flinch.

"Mom! Mom! Mom!" Mini-Jireh One hollers as she wrestles her way out of the tickling onslaught. "Justin pinched me!"

Justin blows a raspberry at his sister. "Mommy! Seeeednee peed on herself!"

Seeeednee gasps. "No. I. Did. Not! You poured apple juice on me!"

Probably on autopilot, Jireh quickly pulls her son over her shoulder by his shirt with one hand and pinches her daughter's cheek with the other. "Sydney, I thought I told you to keep Justin away from the fridge."

"I did!" Sydney exclaims. "But I took some for myself, then he pinched me, and it spilled on me, and then it looked like I peed myself, but of course didn't pee myself, 'cuz I'm seven now, and that's not how it works, but it doesn't matter because I changed by myself and threw the skirt into the dryer, by myself, and Justin is stupid."

"Mommy! Seeeednee called me stupid!" Justin says, fruitlessly struggling like a fish on a hook as Jireh easily holds him in the air.

"Sydney, we agreed that you have to be careful around him," Jireh starts.

"But—"

She turns to her son, who is still trying to get her to let go. "And Justin, me and Sydney are gonna eat all your yogurt tonight."

Justin freezes.

"Cry," Jireh says. "Try me."

Justin doesn't cry.

"Ha, ha!" Sydney taunts, using the opportunity to blow her own raspberry at him.

She immediately stops when she realizes Jireh is staring at her with a raised eyebrow.

"Correction," Jireh says. *"I'll* be eating your yogurt tonight, Justin. And *I* can't wait."

She lets go of him and he lands on the floor in what I'm sure he thinks is a superhero pose.

"But Mooom!" Sydney folds her arms and is about to stomp her foot when Jireh, who is already headed towards the compact kitchen, flicks her fingers and points exactly at her daughter. How she's able to see her is lost on me.

"If you throw a fit I'll send you to the synagogue with grandma tomorrow," she says, fast and terse, like a bullet.

Sydney slowly places her foot on the ground.

"Good girl," Jireh says as she pulls the fabled yogurt out of the fridge. For effect, as she peels open the lid, she takes a full whiff of the treat before reaching behind her to pull out a spoon. Her children stare at her, mouths agape, as she dines on their treat.

Okay, maybe I was wrong. She's being the bad guy here, but I can tell she really is happy. As she smiles devilishly with each spoonful of their strawberry yogurt, I understand this Jireh more and more. She doesn't need her name in lights, or to be a millionaire. She doesn't need a good boss or good coworkers. She doesn't need Jonah, or Momo, or me. She needs Jireh—the old Jireh—and she's got two of those. And despite it still being freaky how there's literally two smaller, louder Jirehs, it's also kind of beautiful in a way, enough to make me fight back tears. A smile finds its way onto my lips. I know she's gonna be just fine.

"Mom, did Uncle Jonah answer today?" Sydney asks as her brother starts climbing up Jireh's legs again.

Jireh seems to deflate, taking my heart with her.

"No, Sydney," she says, placing the half-eaten yogurt on the counter. "Not today."

"Awww, you said he's gonna answer again soon!" Sydney slumps forward a bit, mirroring her mother.

Patting her daughter's head, Jireh smiles as Justin pulls on her hair to get to her shoulders. "He will, I promise."

Justin reaches her shoulders and roars victoriously. "I have slayed the giant!" He wraps his hands around his mother's neck with a little too much vigor.

Jireh once more pulls her son over her shoulder with one arm. "This is why we don't let you watch TV past eight."

She walks out of the kitchen and tosses Justin forward with superhuman strength. He lands on a stained couch about a meter from them.

Maybe it's because I haven't met their father yet—holy shit I wonder who Jireh married—but it's still hard for my brain to accept that these are her kids. If they didn't literally look like the mirror image of her, I'd be inclined to believe she was their babysitter or something.

After tossing the yogurt into the trash can—without looking, I must add—she picks Sydney up like a duffel bag and walks towards a room in the corner.

"Come on, Justin. Bedtime."

Sydney wiggles and giggles underneath her mother's arm. As for Justin, I half expect the little shit to throw a fit, but to my surprise, the opposite happens. His eyes light up with excitement and he runs past them down the hallway, presumably towards the bedroom. Naturally, I follow them.

The bedroom in question is microscopic, with an even tinier bed that somehow takes up more than half of it. In the corner is a plastic drawer with pink tights and a baseball cap poking out.

"This used to be her bedroom, you know," God Two says.

My head tilts. "Okay, I guess? Where does she sleep now?"

He looks at me for a while, then shrugs.

Justin and Sydney get into the bed before making a big show of getting snug under the corners.

Sydney smiles through the gap in her teeth. "Okay, we're ready."

Jireh sits at the edge of the bed and combs her fingers through Justin's hair. Now that I look closely at him, the little stinker looks a lot like Jonah, just with ginger hair instead of black.

"Well..."

"Uncle Jonah!" Justin hollers. "Tell us Uncle Jonah stories!"

Sydney lights up. "Yeah! Pleeeasseee!"

"Pleeeaseee!" Justin joins.

"Pleeeaseee!" they squawk in unison.

"Alright, alright. Stop wailing. I'm going to assume you were joking because there's no way kids of mine are gonna harmonize like that," Jireh says, pinching Justin's cheek.

Sydney's eyebrows furrow as she pouts. "But you said I had a great voice!"

"I lied. Now hush. Do you want an Uncle Jonah story or not?"

"What do you mean you li—"

"Uncle Jonah! Uncle Jonah!" Justin interrupts.

Despite his yelling, I can tell from the way he rubs at his eyes that he's tired.

"Okay, okay. Let me tell you of Uncle Jonah and Uncle Ayo," she starts.

Hold up. Uncle Ayo? Me? I'm Uncle Ayo? That feels... weird. I don't like that. Ugh.

"You see, back then, me, Uncle Ayo, Uncle Jonah, and Aunt Momo were all best friends. We did everything together. Playing video games, watching movies, soccer, you name it. Some of the stuff we did wasn't even things we liked, we just liked doing it with each other—"

"We know, alreadeeee!" Justin hollers through a yawn.

"Aunt Momo's on TV now, right?" Sydney asks.

Momo's on TV? Fuck yeah! She did it!

"Correct. Now one night—wait. How the hell do you know that? Have you been watching TV from behind the couch again? You know what? We'll talk about this later, now hush. Where was I?"

Sydney placed her hand over her brother's snoring mouth. "One night."

"Right, one night, after a sleepover, your uncle and I were sitting in the backyard looking up at the sky. You could see a lot more stars back then. I remember everyone had gone home and it was just me and him. I believe this was a couple weeks before Aunt Momo asked Uncle Ayo out. We were talking and I mentioned this boy I liked, kinda like you and Mrs. Green's kid—"

"Mom! I don't like Mylo! He still eats his boogers and doesn't like *Diary of A Wimpy Kid!*"

"...I remember Uncle Jonah had started to tease me about it. Of course, I couldn't let him get away scott-free, so you know what I said?"

Sydney yawns and shakes her head.

"I asked him who he liked, and he said it was Uncle Ayo."

Pause. My eyes widen into golf balls and I turn to God Two. He doesn't seem surprised by this, and a head turn tells me that neither is God One. How? Since when? Me? Jonah often said he'd fuck anything with a tight enough ass, so it doesn't surprise me that he's into guys. The only issue is that my ass isn't. Tight. My ass isn't tight. So it makes little to no sense that—

"He said he was joking."

Oh.

"But now I know he wasn't. I think he had a massive crush on Uncle Ayo, but you know what he did?"

By now, Sydney is drifting off, but she shakes her head nonetheless.

"Nothing. He knew Uncle Ayo's parents would've given Uncle Ayo so much trouble if they got together, so he let it be. I think that's what happened. He's always been so selfless, even back then. And when Aunt Momo told us she was gonna ask Uncle Ayo out, he didn't even hesitate. He immediately supported her. He always pretended like he didn't care, but he did. He does."

By now both little Jirehs are asleep, but Jireh goes on regardless. Telling herself stories of a Jonah that I never got to fully know, even in four years of high school. I always knew he had a heart somewhere in his chest, it just never occurred to me that it might have had this much room.

I've become completely enraptured in the Jonah saga, and apparently so has Jireh, because when the doorbell rings, both of us jump.

Slowly getting up from the bed, she tiptoes out of the tiny room and walks towards the door, scratching her head.

Without looking through the peephole, Jireh opens the door to come face to face with a man I don't recognize. He's a fairly attractive guy, with blond hair and stubble, gray eyes, and a nervous smile. He's wearing a gray hoodie and sweatpants, clearly here on an impulse decision.

Jireh seems to recognize him, though. She gasps, then her face hardens. "Leave."

"Okay. Yeah, I promised I wouldn't show up again, but in my defense, I was just taking a walk and I saw your car was here earlier than usual, so I thought I'd drop by and say hello."

"You were taking a walk twenty miles from your house?"

He sighs. "She's my daughter, Reh." He looks down when he says this, fiddling with the hem of his hoodie.

"You don't get to call her that," Jireh hisses through her teeth.

He sighs. "I know, and I can't tell you how sorry I am... You know how sorry I am. You know I'm not that guy anymore."

"And?"

He pauses, clearly unable to decide what to say.

"So what if you're not that guy anymore? You *were* that guy. That's all that matters. Now get out."

"Reh, stop."

"Get. Out."

"Reh—"

"Hunter."

"I'm sorry," he finally grunts.

"Fuck you."

"I'm sorry."

"Fuck you."

"I'm sorry."

"Fuck you."

Hunter sighs and combs his hand through his hair. With his eyes closed, I can sort of see the resemblance with Sydney. Thankfully, most of the genetics on that child's face belong to Jireh. I don't know what this fucker did, but I hate him. His face is stupid.

"Look," Hunter says. "The person who did that to you, he's—"

"Say it like it is."

Once more, Jireh's words are like bullets.

"Reh—"

"Say it."

Another sigh. "The guy who took advantage of you—"

"Hunter."

"The guy who..." He winces, then sighs in defeat. "He's dead. I swear I'm not him anymore. I'm not asking you to forgive me, or even to let me be a part of your life again. I'm only asking one day a week. Just one, where I can see my daughter. Because that's what she is! My daughter! I helped create her! We created her!"

"We didn't create her. You shoved her in me. Go to Hell, Hunter."

Jireh slams the door, but Hunter pushes back, stopping it from closing. They stare each other down.

"Please. I'm begging you."

"You didn't seem so eager to have my permission back then."

"Fucking hell, it was eight years ago, Reh! Can't you accept that I'm not that guy anymore?"

"You know what I couldn't do with Sydney in me? Everything. You closed so many doors the day you put that shit in my drink, Hunter. Let me close this one. Go home. And don't fucking come back. Ever."

"No."

"Excuse me?"

"You know damn well you heard me. I've tried, over and over again but you're fucking impossible!"

"I don't owe you a damn thing!"

"No, but I owe her! She needs her father!"

"Then I'll find one! And he'll sure as hell be better than you!"

"Oh my fucking God! You're gonna find one? Can you hear yourself? You sure as hell found one in that piece of shit who 'shoved' Justin in you and dipped last minute!"

She gulps. "How fucking dare you? How do you even know his fucking name?"

"How dare I? Reh, how dare *you*? I can afford to make sure you and those kids never have to lift a finger in your life. Forget child support—which I know for a fact you aren't using, by the way—I could buy you guys an actual fucking home! What school are they going to? What cereal do they eat for breakfast? Do they even have phones? You're withholding so much from your children all because of your fucking ego!"

"It's more than that and you know it!"

"Is it? You let that good-for-nothing Jacob walk in here and knock you up, but you won't let me in, someone who actually wants to FUCKING HELP!"

"AT LEAST JACOB ASKED ME FIRST!"

"WHAT DOES THAT HAVE TO DO WITH—"

"Mom?" Sydney is now behind them, leaning on the doorframe and rubbing her eye. This is when I remember to breathe again.

"Sweetie, go back inside, I'm busy—"

Frantically, before anyone has time to react, Hunter bellows, his words flying like arrows.

"Sydney! I'm your fa—"

With a terrifying force not belonging to someone who used to have Matt and Kim as her alarm, Jireh slams the door in Hunter's face, too swiftly for him to be able to push on it again. Without taking her eyes off her daughter, she locks the door and leans against it.

Silence. Nothing but silence for a few beats.

"Go to bed," she finally whispers.

"Mom, what was that guy saying about—"

"Go to bed." Her voice is a bullet again.

"But—"

"Now, dammit!"

Her face vibrates with the strain of howling each word, and by the time the little girl runs back into her room crying, Jireh is sliding down on the door.

Just as she reaches the ground, her phone rings. She fishes it out and her eyes widen when she sees the caller ID. Frantically, she accepts the call and places the phone to her ear.

"Jonah?" she says, her voice quivering.

My heart freezes.

As quickly as her face lights up, it dies. She pulls the phone away from her ear and hangs her head. Her grip on the device is so viciously tight that her knuckles whiten and her already spiderwebbed phone screen forms more cracks.

I turn to God Two. "What the hell just happened?"

"With the call? Or with everything?"

"With everything, or with the call... I'm—I'm not sure."

God One takes a breath. "Jonah's asking for money."

"Again," God Two adds.

Jireh stands up with a jerk and thrusts the phone away with all her might. It crashes into the wall and the screen with the words "stupiddummybro" shatters into what feels like a million pieces.

I feel a hole form in the pit of my stomach. "Take me to him."

All

I don't think I'll ever get used to being in the white space. The concept of there being no end and no beginning runs circles around me and it requires immense focus to even take a step, as I have no idea where, or even when my foot will land.

"Are you sure you don't want to continue watching?" God Two asks. "She has a talk with Sydney about Hunter, you know."

Despite the fact that I literally have all the time in the world, I shake my head. There's a certain urgency in my desire to see Jonah, and though I can't pinpoint what's causing it, I also can't fight it.

"I need to see Jonah. Please," I say.

God Two nods, and we snap out of the white space. Of course, the sudden shift in my surroundings startles me and I almost land on my ass, if not for God One grabbing hold of my arm.

After I get my bearings, my heart sinks further into my colon. This apartment makes Jireh's look like a condo. The walls are pale blue but feel colorless, and the couch sitting in the corner of the tiny living room is more of a ball of foam and leather than a piece of functioning furniture. The light on the ceiling is so dull it might as well be off, yet it still has the nerve to flicker. As for the carpet, something tells me that once upon a time it was a nice cream color. Now it just looks ill, like it's been vomited on so many times that it itself wants to vomit.

"Where is he?" I croak. My throat is a long, cylindrical desert.

God One points in the direction of an incredibly small hallway, and I swear I'm this close to shitting out my stomach. With tentative feet, I walk down this hallway that's just a few inches wider than my shoulders. The sound of unintelligible muttering bounces off the paper-thin walls, and I take comfort in the fact that it sounds nothing like Jonah's voice.

The hallway has to be only two or three meters long, but it feels like miles before I get to the door at the end. It's slightly ajar, but I phase through it anyways. The brief question of how I'm able to walk on the ground without falling through it swiftly and violently blown away when I see the room.

It's microscopic. Painfully so. The bed is tiny as well, but in this room it might as well be for royalty. On the bed, a man is laying on his back with his eyes cast on nothing, spouting a string of sounds that vaguely resemble English words. He still doesn't sound like Jonah, and he doesn't look like him either, but it doesn't matter. It doesn't matter that there's foam coming out of his mouth, or that I can all but see his skull. It doesn't matter that he has pupils but they aren't being used, or that his hands keep twitching, trying to grab something that isn't there. Nor does it matter that his stubble looks like the aftermath of a wildfire. It doesn't matter because his collars are flipped, and he has a scar under his chin from when we went off-road while biking. It doesn't matter because this *is* Jonah. From the fissures on his tongue that never let him enjoy Nigerian food, to the Mount Everest on his nose, *this* is Jonah.

But this Jonah doesn't make me laugh. He doesn't help me with my essays nor does he teach me the ceaselessly changing rules of D&D. This Jonah is the man under the tree. He is dirt.

The words fly out of my mouth without my permission. "A week. He's better a week from now."

"Ayo—"

"Take me to a week from now! He's better a week from now!"
"Okay, but first—"
My eyelids clench themselves shut. "Do it! Please!"
When my eyes reopen, I'm still in the same room, but now it's empty. I can't say for sure, but that seems to be the only thing that's changed. The sheets are still unkempt and filthy, and the ceiling fan still looks like it's held up with two wires.

I hear voices down the hallway, so faster than I expect, my body turns and heads out the door. This whole day, or week, or however long it's been in me-time since I've been dead feels like a dream. Like an exceptionally vivid, terrifying, joy-filled dream. Fucking hell, I can practically feel Jonah's fingers on my tongue.

Don't cry, Ayo. Don't cry, Ayo. Don't—

"I'm... I'm proud of you," a girl says. She has bright-green eyes and her hair is the color of the sun. It might just be me, but it feels like she's incredibly out of place in this apartment, what with her red sweatpants and black Nike hoodie. Oh God, is she wearing Crocs?

"Thanks, Cassie." I turn to him. Okay, now he looks a little more like Jonah, especially without the foam. His cheeks are still hollow, and his eyes still look like they're about to fall out of their sockets, but at least he has Jonah's signature smirk. *He* is Jonah. He's Jonah.

"How many weeks has it been since..." Cassie asks, fiddling with a pencil in her hand.

The air is heavy with awkwardness, and every word floats in the breeze for a moment before sinking to the ground.

"Eight weeks," Jonah says.

He bites his lip and drums his fingers against the table he's leaning on. He has on a purple flannel over a wife-beater and the rattiest pair of jeans I've ever seen, and his bare feet are somehow ashy enough to be noticeable on his pale skin. Still, he's Jonah.

Hold up. Eight? Is that possible? Unless what we saw before was his withdrawal symptoms? I'm no expert, but I suppose I can see that being the case.

Cassie covers her mouth with her hands and bounces on the balls of her feet. "Oh my God, I can't believe it! I told my mom, and she kept telling me that I should leave you, but I told her that you might actually do it this time and I'm just so happy for you, Jonah I—"

"Thanks, Cassie." He hesitates. His breath is raspy. "I'm sorry that you had to see me... like that." He bites his lip deeper this time.

"Don't apologize. Remember what Meemaw used to say? 'You only find the demons in your closet—'"

"'—When you decide to change your clothes,'" Jonah finishes. His smile is wispy, like a moment's wind might wipe it away. Still, it's there. "How is she anyways?"

Cassie's grin fades. "She...She passed away. Last month."

Jonah's eyes widen and his breath hitches. "What? Why... Why didn't you tell me?"

Now it's Cassie's turn to bite her lip. "I tried. Multiple times. You never picked up, Jonah."

"Oh."

"Yeah."

"I'm... I'm really sorry to hear that, Cassie. I loved Meemaw."

"It's fine, she didn't suffer. She went in her sleep, and that's something we can be grateful for, I guess."

"Yeah, of course."

"I'm just happy to see you, Jonah. I missed you like crazy! Can I hug you?"

He barely has time to nod before Cassie barrels into his arms, squeezing him so hard I worry this frail form he has might shatter. She pulls away after a good ten seconds before leaning up to kiss his forehead. It feels weird watching them, like I'm spying on something private. Which I suppose I am, but what good are morals when one is dead?

Cassie pulls away, and her face is bright pink. Her smile is radiant, and her eyes do a better job of lighting up the place than the bulb still flickering on the ceiling. "I know it's been really hard, but I was talking to Dr.Robertson and she said that healing isn't a linear process. You're going to be fine, Jonah. I swear." She sniffs. "Have you been eating ramen?"

The wispy smile returns to his face. "Religiously."

"Jonah," she chastises.

He chuckles and shrugs, "Ramen's cheap, what do you want from me?"

Cassie's smile fades. "Can you not afford real food?" she asks. Her mouth twitches.

"Cass, it's—"

She doesn't hesitate. Reaching into the pockets of her red sweatpants, Cassie pulls out her wallet and whips out a bunch of cash notes without even looking.

"Cass, I can't…"

His demeanor has changed. His hand is twitching, his breath has hastened, and his eyes will look anywhere but at Cassie. "Cass, please don't give me that—"

"What are you talking about? You need actual food in your system if you're gonna get any better—"

It's his arm that dashes out and rips the cash from her fingers, but it doesn't look like it was his intent to do so. His arm is vibrating, like he's trying to make it drop the money with all his might, but it won't let him.

Cassie seems to have realized what she's done, because her eyes widen and her lower lip quivers.

"Jonah," she cautiously says, like she's talking to a wild animal. "You're gonna take that money and you're gonna go to Walmart and buy groceries, right? To cook?"

Jonah says nothing. His teeth bite his lower lip and his eyes stare at his feet.

My heart is screaming. Who the fuck is this Cassie bitch? His girlfriend? There's no way he could have fallen far enough to date someone stupid enough to give money to a recovering addict! What the fuck is her problem? Now she's standing there looking like she's about to cry, like she wasn't the one who put him in danger in the first place!

My face must mirror my thoughts, because God Two rests his hand on my right shoulder. "You look angry. You alright?"

"How can I not be angry? This bitch just straight up gave money to a recovering addict! Who the hell does that?! God knows what he's gonna do with that money now. Goddamnit—"

I stop. My throat is choking up and I don't want to cry. I breathe.

"He might go off the deep end and it's going to be her fault."

"Is that how that works?" God One, interjects. His hands are in his pockets as usual, but his eyes are trained on Cassie's expression. "She trusted him, and he failed."

"She's an idiot. Giving him that money was a mistake," I scoff.

Don't cry, Ayo. Don't cry, Ayo.

Cassie gulps audibly. "Jonah, you're gonna get actual food, right? Pizza, maybe?" Her voice begins to tremble. "You're gonna get something substantial and you're gonna eat, right? Tell me you're gonna eat!"

He tries. I swear to fucking God Jonah tries to talk, but it won't let him, and it pounds and twists something in my chest until it breaks. It hurts even more because I know what I feel is nothing compared to what he's feeling.

"JONAH!" Cassie screeches.

Tears fall from his eyes. They gush in droves. When I died, only one managed to get through his gates, but now, they're all pouring out. There are no gates left. The ones he used to have must have broken, and now there isn't enough in him to build anymore. So he just stands there, weeping, fighting his body as Cassie screams at him. This isn't Jonah. This pathetic husk of a man isn't Jonah. I don't know what piece is missing from his puzzle, but it's big enough to make him something else. Something unrecognizable. Something even he is afraid of.

Fuck, my chest.

"Jonah… give me that money. Now."

Cassie reaches for it, but he moves backwards. This is the only time his body acknowledges her, so it takes all three of us by surprise.

Cassie's face contorts in rage, and she grabs his arm. I think she genuinely thought that would work, because her expression turns to utter shock when Jonah snatches her hand and flings her away like a piece of plastic. She stumbles, lands on her ass, and looks at Jonah the way you look at someone vaguely familiar. Like she's trying to pinpoint who exactly she's looking at and where she's seen him before. It's the same look my mother gave my father the night I died.

She appears to give up, because she stands up, brushes the dust off of her pants and turns to leave. On her way out, she stops at a picture on the wall by the door. Oh God. It's me and him, a picture we took when I blacked out from drinking for the first time. Momo and Jireh were scared shitless, but Jonah just took a bunch of selfies with me making several expressions. In this one, he was using his fingers to pucker my lips and placed his cheek against it. I can't believe he kept that, much less framed it.

"He'd be disappointed in you. You know that? He'd see you and he'd spit," Cassie spat. Her voice is barely recognizable under the choked-back sobs.

Jonah says nothing.

"I'm sorry," she backtracks.

Jonah says nothing.

She leaves.

Jonah sits in silence, eventually unclasping his fingers as he looks at the money.

"Me too," he whispers. He then puts on his slides and trudges out the door.

I want to follow him. God, I want to follow him. But I can't. I've seen enough to be afraid of what I might see.

"Where's he going?" I ask God Two.

He removes his hand from my shoulder; I'd honestly forgotten it was there. "He's going to—"

"Roverwood Rehabilitation Center," God One says.

My heart leaps. "You mean—"

"He's going to walk in front of the building, and stare at it for two hours before walking away. Like he's done everyday, for the past two years."

Oh.

God One pulls out a cigarette and lights it, presumably with his mind or some shit. "The staff know him, and he's actually made friends with the janitor. They're even on a first name basis," He places the magic cigarette in his mouth, takes a whiff, and pulls it out.

"Except Jonah thinks his name is Bob, for some reason. Despite the fact that 'Bob' has told him multiple times that it's Reggie. Now he just accepts it. It's kinda cute, actually."

My face heats up. Fast. "You think this is a joke?" I ask through my teeth.

God One finally looks at me before blowing magic smoke in my face. "You can get angry at that Cassie chick all you want, but it doesn't change the fact that she believed he could control himself, and he lied. It might not be something he can help, but he chose this path instead of crying like everybody else. Now the sorry son of a bitch can't do anything *but* cry." He blows smoke in my face again. "That's who he is. That's the kind of man he is."

"That's not Jo—"

"When are you gonna understand? There is no past, present, or future anymore. Not for you. That *is* Jonah, that *was* Jonah, and that *will be* Jonah. Frozen in place for you to see over and over again until you decide you want to move on to something else. Accept it. This is Jonah."

"After he leaves the building, he's going to walk two miles to get to a man's car, spend twenty minutes in there, and come out with his pockets full," God Two says.

I gulp. "What happens then?"

He says nothing. Instead, he flicks his fingers and the light coming through the smudged-to-shit windows instantly dims as though he's turned the light switch off on the universe.

Jonah stumbles in like a tired and sweaty hurricane and collapses on what I keep assuming is supposed to be a sofa. The side of his face firmly planted in the foam, he pulls out his phone and taps a few times before the other end starts ringing. It rings, and rings, and rings, but no one picks up. I can't say how, but I know it's Jireh, and

I'm pretty sure a cracked phone screen isn't why she's not answering.

Then, his phone dings and his face lights up like a Christmas tree. It's a voice message. He taps on it and in New-Jireh or I guess Jireh-Jireh's firm, somewhat angry voice, a row of words shoot out.

"Go to fucking Roverwood, Jonah."

They slap him in the face and turn into dead silence. Each word a bullet.

In that silence, Jonah whispers, so weak and so quiet that I doubt he knows he said it out loud.

"But I'm trying…"

A lone tear gets past my gate, prompting me to stiffen up. I wipe it off. This isn't my fight. I have no right to cry here or to hurt for him, but *fuck*, man. What the hell happened to him?

I stand there and watch him for what must be close to an hour. He does nothing, he says nothing. He might as well be dead.

Eventually, he rolls off of the couch and lands on the floor with a thud and a groan. There's no fight left in him as he pulls a plastic bag with syringes in it out of his pocket. Jonah coughs, then pulls one out just as the doorbell rings.

He seems to contemplate whether or not it's worth getting up, but eventually he half-heartedly drops the syringe back into the bag and shoves said bag under the couch.

Then he gets to his feet and slogs to the door. He doesn't even get there before it's opened by the person outside and a woman stares at him with a mischievous smile on her face. Her hair is white now, and she's wearing actual make-up, but I know her. I know her because she's mine.

Still, my heart leaps into my throat, because I don't know what I'll do to myself if she isn't.

OF

"Yes or yes," Momo says, leaning against the doorway. "You have molly."

Jonah sighs. "Good evening to you too, Momo."

Holy shit. *Holy* shit! It's Momo. It's *fucking* Momo! And she looks great! Her new hair color is fantastic, and she somehow looks even taller, though it might just be her heels. She's wearing this gorgeous white coat over a maroon halter top, and ripped jeans. She's dressed like a different person, but it looks great on her, as everything does. Her smile is as perfect as ever, though, so much so that it almost feels like she shouldn't be allowed to exist. Like an unbalanced character in a video game, she's perfect, and a massive part of me wants to reach out to hug her, even though I know it'll be futile.

It's weird, because I thought I'd already accepted that I couldn't go back, but seeing her like this makes me wish with every part of me that I could have been less of an idiot. I miss her. I miss everyone.

"How many times have I asked you to stop coming to me for ecstasy?" Jonah huffs. He almost sounds like himself for a moment.

Momo walks past him and beelines for what I'm inclined to believe is a kitchen. She swings open the fridge, not even flinching when it makes an awful screeching sound on its hinges. She then pulls out a bottle of whisky and pops off the cap with her teeth. I watch the love of my life gulp down a quarter of the bottle in one go and release what is possibly the biggest burp I've ever heard. She's ruder, but this is Momo. That belch confirms it.

"God, I love cheap whisky," she says after a sigh. "Anyway, what were you saying?"

"Get an actual dealer."

"No."

He sighs and rubs his forehead. "What the hell do you need that shit for?"

"What the hell does anyone use molly for?" Momo asks as she sifts through his barren cupboard. "Sex."

"You come to me for this shit every week. How much sex are you having?"

Momo pulls out a virtually empty bag of Doritos and dumps the crumbs into her mouth. "Well that's an inappropriate question to ask a lady."

Jonah just stares at her.

"Okay." She sighs. "I have a lot of sex."

Jonah just stares at her.

"With a lot of people."

Still staring.

"At once."

Jonah walks towards the door and opens it.

"Oh come oooonnn!" she whines. "Pleeeaseeee? I promise I'll—"

Hold up. Did she—

How could—

My chest. It's eating me from the inside. Fuck. Fuck, fuck, *fuck*. Yes, it's unreasonable for me to not expect Momo to have sex with other people. It's literally been a decade, but shit. That hurts. Of course I don't want her to be miserable over me, but... I don't know. I guess I'm just jealous of the guy—er, guys. That's stupid, I know. I wish I didn't feel this way. But the drumming of my chest and the heat behind my ears don't ask me for my consent. Fuck! I should have looked both wa—

"Tell you what," Jonah says, lazily closing the door. His use of his arms show them shaking, just in case I forgot that this is my Jonah. "I'll give you what you're asking for if, and only if, you…"—he gulps—"you pay me."

Momo blinks. "Huh?"

"Did I stutter?"

"No, sorry. It's just you usually take my friendship as payment."

"Yeah, well, I need something actually useful this time."

"Ha! I'm a little drunk right now, so I'll let that slide." She reaches into her pocket and pulls out her wallet.

"You must be broke as fuck, huh?" She chuckles, but it dies once she notices how fast Jonah has traversed the apartment and appeared in front of her.

"Jeez." She laughs nervously as she pulls out a couple hundred bills like it's nothing. "You been working out?"

Jerkily, he sweeps the cash from her fingertips and it lands in his pocket within a second.

"Crossfit." His gaze is writhing, but it won't reach hers. Her forehead or her chin, sure, but not her eyes. Not once.

He walks past her and pushes the rusty fridge out of the way before pulling out a floorboard.

"How much did you give me?"

"Uh, I don't know. Like, five hundred?"

Jonah pulls out a plastic bag with about twenty or thirty sky-blue pills. He tosses it to Momo, who catches it without thinking as he puts the floorboard back and pushes the fridge over it, grunting breathlessly the whole time.

"You know, I never asked, but"—Momo places the bag in her coat—"how the hell can you afford this shit?"

"I bought a bunch a couple months ago when I wasn't as strapped for cash—"

"You mean with the money I lent you?"

"—and I just kept 'em, I guess. They're mainly for you since molly's not really my thing."

"Awww! You really do care about me, don't you?" She hugs him from behind with a shit-eating grin. "I love you too, Jonah."

"Alright, get out," he says. Though he makes no effort to shake her off, his lips actually quiver when she lets go.

"Alright, Jonah, I'll see you—"

"Wait!" he says. His voice is shaking, as are his hands and eyes.

Momo stops and turns to him. "You good, Jonah?"

"D-don't leave me alone with it..." He whispers, but it's deafening.

Momo doesn't ask him to repeat himself, nor does she ask who "it" is. Instead, she follows Jonah's gaze to the poorly hidden bag of syringes underneath the couch.

Wordlessly, she walks over there, bends down, and picks up the bag. A few seconds of inspection later, she pockets it. As she turns around, Momo jumps as Jonah, who has once more managed to traverse the apartment in the blink of an eye, appears next to her. His arm grabs Momo's.

"What the? I thought you—"

"It won't let you," he says through his teeth.

Momo's eyes widen as she realizes "it" wasn't the pills.

"Jonah, let me go."

That's when I notice how tight his grip is. His arm is shaking, veins twist around his forearm, and I'm honestly surprised Momo isn't wincing at all. She's glaring instead. Which seems to take both me and Jonah by surprise.

Jonah stares back at her, his lips unsteady. "I can't—"

"You're fucking sick. Now let go, you're hurting me."

"I said, I can't."

"Let me go, Jonah Eddison, or so help me, God."

Fuck. She *has* changed, she's still Momo, I haven't lost faith in that yet. But she's... less shiny. She radiates just a little less light now, and it almost stings of betrayal. I don't think I've ever seen Momo get this angry, especially at a friend. And threatening him? Momo would never do that! What the hell happened to these people?

"Look, I want to, believe me, but—"

"But you can't? Are you fucking kidding me? You're a grown-ass man, just let me fucking go! I probably paid for this shit anyway."

"No, it was Cass."

Momo's eyebrows spike. "Fucking *Cassie*?! You're using that girl's money for this shit?"

His gaze drops even further.

"What's wrong with you?" She struggles against him, but his grip won't budge.

"I don't even know what kind of drug you must have given that sweet girl for her to still stay with you."

Somehow, his grip tightens. This time Momo does wince. "Don't compare me to Hunter!"

Her eyebrows furrow. "Who?"

"N- nevermind, just leave Cassie out of this."

"Why? You didn't! Besides, dumb bitch must have been dumber than I thought if she gave your twitching ass money!"

No. No, no, no, no, *no*. This is all wrong. Why is this all wrong?

"Hey! Why are you so angr—"

"LET ME GO, JONAH! I'm taking this shit with me! I'm not letting you run yourself into the FUCKING GROUND!"

"Listen, I—"

"'LET ME GO!" Now Momo has become the wild animal. She's thrashing around, screaming as she tries to get him to let her go. Jonah is shocked by this, but his arm still won't release her. Even after Momo bites it.

"I SAID LET GO, DAMMIT!"

"Jesus, calm down!"

"I'M TAKING THIS SHIT WITH ME!"

"NO!"

"TRY AND STOP ME!" Her eyeliner is running down her face, her lipstick paints her chin, and her hair is a bird's nest. She looks rabid. Yet, I have to remind myself this is the Momo I know. She's *my* Momo.

Don't cry, Ayo. Don't cry.

With an ear-piercing screech, Momo goes in for another bite, but I watch Jonah's free arm leave his side, swipe across the distance between his leg and Momo's face before finally slamming into her cheek. In that fraction of a second, her skin ripples from the impact and her eyes squint shut.

The sound is definite. It glares at the two of them and dares any one of them to speak. They comply, and the world freezes. Time does not pass as they stare each other down, and the air is so heavy that my lungs struggle to find any.

Jonah lets go of Momo.

Still staring at him, she puts her hand in her pocket, pulls out the bag, and dumps it at his feet. Some of the syringes spill out.

"You know I don't even use ecstasy, right?"

Jonah gulps. "What?"

She looks at the bag on the floor. "I have a net worth of about ninety million dollars, give or take. I can quite literally go wherever and do whatever I want with ease, and yet the highlight of my week is buying drugs I don't need from that guy I knew in high school."

Her gaze goes back to Jonah. "Pick it up."

With quivering hands, Jonah crouches and puts the syringes back into the bag. He handles them gently, like they're pieces of glass, or priceless artifacts, or memories.

While picking up syringes, he finally looks up at Momo, who glares icicles at him through moist eyes.

"If you're going to leave me," she hisses, "at least pull the band-aid off all at once."

After that she turns and heads towards the door. On her way out, she stops and stares at the photo of Jonah and me.

"I want to say he'd vomit, but I don't think he would." Her voice finally begins to waver as she continues. "I think the son of a bitch would actually feel bad for you." She opens the door and leaves, but she whispers something. I hear her, though, and I'm sure Jonah does too.

"Maybe that's why I loved him."

"Ayo," God Two whispers to me. His hand finds its way around my shoulder, "We can go somewhere else, you know. You're not obligated to watch this."

I try to gulp, but there's a boulder in my throat.

"I know," I croak, "but—"

Jonah jerks up, and damn near runs down the hall to his bedroom. Rustling bounces off the walls before he comes back out with a belt and sinks into his couch. Biting his lip to stop its quivering, he wraps the belt around his biceps, pulling it taut with his teeth.

He begins beating himself, viciously grunting as he slams his palm against his arm over and over again. I don't want to cry, so I shut my eyes and shield my ears with my hands… but I still hear him.

I still hear him.

The grunting stops and I can almost hear him sigh in relief.

Don't cry, Ayo.

The sound of plastic landing on the floor. It's hollow.

Don't cry.

He sighs again. And again.

Don't.

And then he whispers—

"Too many stories…"

"*…and not enough happy endings.*" I hear him say it. I swear to God I hear him say it, but the voice belongs to the ghost of whom he used to be.

Part 3

For My Bubble Of Stars

Them

God One, God Two, and I stare at Jonah. He's writhing on the floor, grasping for stars that aren't there, and laughing at jokes that no one made. It's almost haunting to know that he's experiencing a whole different world that I'll never be able to see.

My thoughts drift to Momo and how much angrier she is. She's crasser, ruder, and somehow wittier, but she hasn't changed the way Jireh and Jonah have. Jireh used to be a flower, the kind of girl that cried at the opening credits of a movie with a sad instrumental. Now she's a rock, and as much as that sounds like an improvement, my glimpse into her life tells me it's not without its holes.

As for Jonah, he used to be a constant source of laughter for me. His deadpan, impassive reaction to everything made for such relaxing conversations, and some of the words he's said to me will probably stay with me for the rest of my li— eternity. For the rest of my eternity. He was the kind of guy that made you think you had good luck just from meeting him. But now, as he's pointing at his pitiful lightbulb and licking his lips, he's barely even a person.

And me, what kind of person would I have been if I'd kept pace with them that night? Truthfully, I don't know. I didn't have any real direction in life, so if anything, I'd be the worst of the bunch. I want to say that Jonah would still be the same if I had survived, but then I remember what God One said about him choosing this instead of weeping like everyone else, and I'm not so sure. I hope, and I hope, but I can't lie to myself. Not about this. It's quite possible that me and my stupidity broke Jonah, and all I had to do was look both ways.

"Take me to Momo," I tell the gods, because she's gonna be fine. She's going to be fine.

God Two snaps his fingers and suddenly we're on the sidewalk of a fairly busy street. It's just as rundown as the apartment we were just in, with graffiti on the governing walls and people draped in barely-there clothing walking back and forth, all reeking of rejection. It seems like the place dying things would crawl into to cling to life. It was—

"Oh shit, really?!"

The sudden noise erupting from my left makes me jump. I turn to see Momo talking obnoxiously loud on her phone, not at all acting like someone who'd just told their best friend to kill themself, or like a popular, attractive, young woman in a street that looked just about ready to swallow her up.

"Yeah, yeah, my Uber just turned the corner. I'm on my way." She removes the phone from her ear and immediately the smile drains from her face. She still doesn't look at all worried about where she is or the strange looks she's getting. She just looks angry. Like she wants to spit.

A car pulls up in front of her and the passenger window rolls down. "Uh... are you Momo Sayuri?"

He's a fan, you can tell. That, or Momo is just famous enough that you don't need to be a fan to get flustered. Didn't she say she had ninety million dollars? Jesus Christ. I knew she could do it.

"Yeah, hon. Are you my Uber?" She's back to all smiles, and it's so quick I do a double take. I've known she was a talented actress for years, but to see that skill being used so quickly and so practically is almost scary. Momo's as powerful as ever, I suppose.

She gets in the passenger seat after the guy nods, and without asking, God Two snaps us into the back seat of the car just as it begins to move.

"So what's someone like you doing in a neighborhood like… this?" the guy asks, his hands nervously drumming against the steering wheel as he damn near zooms out of the area.

Momo folds her legs on the dashboard. "Molly," she says, pulling a stick of gum out of her coat.

"Oh."

"Want some?"

"No thanks, heh. I'll be driving for pretty much the whole day."

Momo turns her head and quizzically stares at him. As she blows a bubble she begins poking his cheek with her index finger.

Poke, poke, poke.

Her bubble pops.

"I was referring to gum," she says with a wispy smile. Like the breeze coming through the windows might sweep her away at any given moment.

"Oh, yeah sure." He chuckles, and I can tell he's berating himself right now.

"What was your name again?" Momo says, as she pulls out another strip of gum from her coat.

"Jaco—" He clears his throat. "Jacob."

"Ah." She hands him the stick of gum. "Well, thanks for the ride, Jacob. I'm going to sleep the rest of the way there, if you don't mind."

"Oh no, you're fine."

"Shit."

"What?"

"I probably should've asked before I put my fucking feet on your dash."

"Oh. Well, that's fine too. I can easily clean it."

Momo closes her eyes. "Nah, remind me when we get there to give you an extra tip, Jacob."

"Oh, wow! Thanks!" he exclaims, not realizing she's already asleep.

I've been stupid for as long as I can remember, but it's not hard to tell that some of the gears in Momo aren't ticking anymore. I've said it before and I'll say it again: she's still Momo, but now I realize that perhaps a part of her... isn't. Holes have a way of making themselves known, even if they're littering a person who put forever in the palm of my hand.

I turn to God Two, my heart pounding in my ears. "Wherever she's going, take me there, please."

His smile doesn't match his eyes as he flicks his fingers, but before I can ponder what's wrong, we're somewhere else and everything comes flooding towards me at once.

The switch is made even more disorienting by the deafening music bouncing off of my chest and onto the walls. Lights run across the ceiling, floors, faces, and people. People are everywhere. Arms flail across my face and a bunch of girls run through me and the gods. It's too much at once. It's too fast, too loud, and it's—shit. I can't breathe. I can't—

We're in the white space.

"What did you—"

"Ayo. We can stop, you know?" God Two says. His eyes are warm, yet they pierce right through me.

"No, I'm fine. Don't worry about it."

"I just don't see the point of getting hurt! You're no longer a part of this world and you can go anywhere you want! There's no point in hurting any—"

"Stop. Momo's fine. Stop talking like that."

God One rolls his eyes. "Don't be an idiot. He's doing this for—"

"It's fine," God Two says. "Let's take him to her. We owe him that much."

I blink. "Y-you owe me?"

We snap back into the club. Once again, the switch from an empty space to one with so much happening at once is shocking, but I just manage to keep my shit together. Of course, this is no longer the case a few moments later. I'm about to vomit my heart out when I see her. It's the clothes I recognize first, but then I realize that it's the lights that make her white hair look purple.

Momo is dancing like she's the only one in the room, and it's not long before she spins in my direction and I'm almost frozen by her beauty. How the hell does she still look the same? Her face is firmer, sure, but she's probably like, twenty-eight and looks like she's barely over twenty. Once more, her smile stabs something in my chest, and that ball that appears in your throat when you're about to cry shoves its way up into mine. I missed this. I missed *her*. She's had a whole decade of life, loves, hates, tears, and laughter, and I missed those, too. All of it. Fuck.

A girl with blood-red hair runs to Momo and wraps her arm around her. Her arm is holding a phone and the flashlight tells me they're about to take a selfie. Then a brunette pops out of the ether and presses her face against Momo's and does that duckface thing.

Momo doesn't hesitate. She smiles widely and raises a peace sign. After the selfie is taken, all three jump into conversation. I move through the crowd (literally) to get to them. I want—ah, who am I kidding? I *need* to hear her voice again.

"Oh my God, Bree!" Momo is still an excellent shouter, it seems. "I genuinely think he's doing it to fuck with me!"

The brunette, Bree, gasps. "Really?"

"Why else would his breath smell that bad *only* during the kissing scenes?"

"I don't know." The redhead twirls and places her hands on Momo's shoulders. They start moving together, and Bree's eyebrows furrow.

"I feel like kissing him would be worth it, though!"

Bree places her chin on Momo's shoulder. Momo wraps her arms around Bree's shoulders and turns to her.

"Would you look at that?" Bree says. Her hands are now on Momo's waist; she's stolen the dance. "Amber's being a whore, who's surprised?"

A series of thoughts and emotions seem to run through Amber's eyes. She takes Momo's hand and twirls her. The dance is now hers again.

"Trust me. it's not worth it! The guy's a piece of shit!" Momo doesn't seem to know or care that they're playing ping pong with her, but I do. It almost feels like a slap in the face, because even though I know it isn't the case, it feels like she's replaced gold with plastic.

God, I sound like a jackass.

"Yeah, you're right! He's got a seedy look to him!" Amber dips and catches Momo, and their laughter feels plastic too.

Joining on the laughter, Bree pulls Momo in for another selfie and Amber scrambles to join in. After this one, something seems to shift in Momo. Her dances gradually get tamer and tamer until she stops. She stands there, body and mind numb, watching the world moving around her. She absorbs the music, the lights, the sweat, the laughter, and the vibrations on the floor from all the dancing. And I see it. With my own two eyes, I see her become like me. She's watching the world revolve around her and she's shrinking. It's clear then: Momo Sayuri doesn't belong here any more than I do.

People seem to notice her for the first time, and it isn't long before a crowd forms. Some ask for selfies, some take one without asking, some ask her if she can "hook them up", and others get lost in the rush. Momo does nothing. She just stares at them, blinking like she can't hear what they're saying. As for Amber and Bree, they make no move to help her. Instead, they're reveling in it, taking pictures with people who know them by association and answering questions they don't seem to know the answers to. The whole thing is a mess.

"I'm gonna get some fresh air!" Momo suddenly says, pointing towards the door.

"Oh no!" Amber cups her face, and behind Momo, Bree's nose scrunches. "Are you okay?"

"Yeah, I'm fine. Just give me a minute." She slightly jostles her way towards the exit, and I follow her. With each step, her pace quickens until she's all but shoving people out of her way in her bid to get out. Eventually, she bursts through the door and turns to face the brick wall beside it.

It's night time now, and the rain is pouring so hard it feels like the city is weeping. Momo's hands are planted against the wall and she's panting. Her body rises and falls with each breath.

"Fuck, fuck, FUCK!" she says. "What the fuck is wrong with me?! Okay, Momo. You can do it. You can do it. You can…"

Apparently she can't, because she sighs and turns to rest her back on the wall. She slides down until she reaches the ground and looks up at the sky, squinting against the rain.

"Hey, Ayo."

My breath catches.

"It's been a minute, huh? I used to talk to you all the time… I guess seeing you in Jonah's hit me different, you know? Anyway, I'm… I'm trying, man. I swear, I'm trying. Did the college shit with

Jireh just like we planned, made a shit ton of money, and I still have my whole career in front of me." She takes a shaky breath. "But you know what? I miss jollof rice. I'll be honest I never used to like it when I ate it at your place back then, but I fucking miss jollof rice, man. It was good shit." Her voice is unrecognizable. "I miss it. I miss it so much." A sob makes its way out of her. "It's been ten FUCKING years! I've moved on, I swear, it's just... I don't want it to happen again... and it's gonna happen again. You're gonna happen again." Now she's openly weeping. "And I fucking miss jollof rice, dammit."

The way she says I'm going to "happen again" hits me hard. Like I'm not—I wasn't—her boyfriend, but some natural disaster. As if my entire being has been enveloped in the pain that my death brought her.

"Do you get it now? You don't have to watch this," God Two says.

I can't see him though, not through the tears I won't let fall.

"No," I say, wiping my eyes. "She's had a shitty day, cut her some sla—"

"Oh for fuck's sake!" God One snaps.

I turn to him, and to my surprise he doesn't look angry. Rather, it's the same kind of look my father would give me when he was trying to help me with my math homework. Okay, never mind. He's definitely angry.

"She's. Fine," I say through my teeth.

Without breaking eye contact with me, he snaps his fingers. Our environment drastically switches, the rain stops, sunbeams shoot through window panes, and we're in some kind of office with plain, beige walls save for a few plaques and photo frames here and there. In front of a desk, in two couches parallel to one another, Momo sits facing a blond woman with glasses, wearing a green knit sweater and a black pencil skirt.

Momo sighs, her voice is tiny. Barely even there. "This… this morning I…" She takes a shaky but tired breath, like she's trying to push the words out but they're too heavy.

She breathes. "I googled how long it takes to drown."

I can't help it. I try, I swear to God almighty I try, but it's impossible. My floodgates shatter, and the tears don't bother asking before they burst through.

To

Momo's therapist is called Dr. Heather. I know this because she's the one Momo made me go to after I hurt myself. Unlike Momo, Dr. Heather has in fact aged. The lines on her face have lengthened, and several strips of her blonde hair have turned white. As for her smile, it's as warm as ever, and my hatred for it hasn't softened in the least.

"What do you think led you to looking that up, Momo?" she asks, looking up from her notepad and interlocking her fingers over her crossed knee.

"Um... well, I was at The Halo and the glass wall thing happened again." Momo picks at an imaginary fabric on her coat, not meeting Dr. Heather's gaze. She's wearing the same clothes she wore with Jonah and in the club, except now her hair is somehow messier. And even with her makeup now wiped off, she still doesn't look twenty-eight.

Dr. Heather leans forward. "You're gonna have to give me more than that, Momo."

Momo groans and slumps back into the couch. "Ugh, you always ask me that!"

"And I'm content with the sarcastic deflections, but this is a new development. Looking up information like that is serious." She uncrosses her legs and shifts forward. "Come on, tell me."

She smiles and I bite the inside of my cheek on instinct. Coming here was always the worst part of my week. Not because Dr.

Heather wasn't kind or well intentioned, far from it. It's just how warm her character was. It felt like opening the window to let sunlight in on a bunch of dead plants. When you're in a rut, positivity doesn't pull you out, it reminds you how far you've fallen.

Apparently, Momo doesn't seem to share my sentiment, because, unlike me, she stares at the ceiling, and says, "I guess, the glass wall is this... well, wall, that separates me from everyone else. I can see them, and I can sort of hear them, but all their words come out muffled, stilted even. And as for *my* words, most of the time they don't even hear them at all. Like I'm talking and they're not listening. They're just looking at me like I'm a goddamn animal exhibit.

"And it's crazy, 'cuz I know a part of them hears me. They know I'm saying something, but it's like they just don't want to believe I'm a human being because I'm the tall chick on TV with the tits. God for-fucking-bid I go to fucking McDonald's on a Saturday night. And it's not like I'm a diva or whatever! I say and ask for simple shit, but it's like they're not hearing me! Am I even here?! Why won't they listen?! No, I don't want to work with Caleb Belle, he's a fucking creep. Yes, I would like two tickets to see Mission Impossible. No, I don't want honey mustard with that. I don't *like* honey mustard. Why the fuck do you keep staring at me? Can you not hear the words coming out of my mouth? Stop putting the FUCKING HONEY MUSTARD IN THE FUCKING BAG YOU JUST HEARD ME SAY I DON'T LIKE HONEY MUSTARD!"

Momo freezes, then looks around like it's taking her brain a moment to register where she is. She swallows, but you can tell from the slight wince on her face that there isn't a drop of moisture in her mouth.

"Sorry," she whispers. "Got a little heated there."

Dr. Heather does something she never did with me. She puts her notebook to the side and leans forward even more.

"You seem to have put a lot of thought into this, Momo."

"Too much thought, probably. And it isn't like this is just because I'm famous or whatever. I've felt some version of this ever since I was a kid. It's just that, back then, there were fewer people on the other side of the glass and more on mine. People would gawk at my height or whatever, but if I talked loud enough, if I yelled in their faces enough, eventually they'd hear me. Now..."

"Now they don't want to hear you."

Momo looks down. "Now they don't want to hear me. Some nights it's more of a steel wall, if anything. I don't know, maybe I'm blowing this all out of proportion, but—"

"Don't dismiss your feelings. They're real, they're legitimate, and though they're intangible, they more than make up for that in the tangible effect they have on your life."

As I'm standing here having my world rocked at the realization that she and I were this alike, Momo remains silent. She then sits up and fixes her gaze on Dr. Heather. Her eyes are hard. "The other day, I did something I haven't done since college. Do you remember Ayo?"

Dr. Heather purses her lips. "Yes."

"Well, I... I talked to him."

"Do you want to share what you said?"

"I told him what was going on and how I felt at that stupid club... and that I missed jollof rice. That last part was dumb."

"Do you often find yourself missing Ayo?"

"...Kind of. It's crazy 'cuz I don't think about him the way I used to. In the early years after he died, not a day would pass that I wouldn't think about him, and most mornings I'd wake up and have this insane craving to just hold him... and I'd just cry because I couldn't. Now I can go whole weeks without thinking of him, usually with help, mind you, but the point is I've moved on. I know I have. I've had a shit ton of boyfriends since he died. Some of them were frankly better partners than he was, and one I think I actually loved more than I did Ayo… and yet, I always seem to find myself coming back to him."

My knees and my head and my stomach are jello, but no longer because of shock. I knew this would happen from even before I died. The fact that I'm a footnote in their lives has never been lost on me, but it's one thing to see something with your head, and another to see it with your eyes. Momo has moved on. She's loved more, laughed more, and lived more, but all with me pulling her back from growing like she should—

"You're wrong," God Two says. "You left her with far more than just sadness."

I turn to him. "Then why is she hurting? Tell me why she's hurting!"

He hesitates. "Perhaps *because* you left her with more than sadness."

"What the fuck does that—"

"Momo," Dr. Heather says, leaning back into her chair and picking her notebook back up. "Maybe it's time to find new friends. Ones who actually listen."

Momo snickers, but it's void of humor. "In this industry, you can't really tell who listens from who pretends to."

"What about your old friends? You guys used to be so close."

"Well, Ayo got clapped and Jonah might as well be clapped."

"Don't you think you're being a little insensitive?"

Momo shrugged. "And as for Jireh, we don't talk anymore."

Dr. Heather reads my mind. "May I ask why?"

Again, Momo sighs. "When you get as big as me as fast as I did, you're suddenly hit with a wave of people who said 'hi' to you at a Starbucks and now think it's okay to ask for money or clout. So when, a couple years back, Jireh texted me for the first time in years, asking me for some money, I got mad and... and well I kind of ghosted her. And I'm more reasonable now, I swear. I give Jonah money all the time, but I just never called Jireh back. We haven't seen or talked since. Even after I moved out of Los Angeles."

Momo is playing with her fingers, avoiding Dr. Heather's gaze. As selfish as it may be, the urge to pull her out of this world and into mine is overbearing. But unfortunately, holding her and shielding her from the ugliness is something I couldn't do, dead or alive. Even if I could, there's more than just a world separating us.

"Perhaps we should start there, then." Dr. Heather puts her notepad to the side and comes to sit next to Momo. "Listen to me, Momo. I'm telling you this not as your therapist, but as a friend of the family. You've got to come back to the ground. To the places and things that made you, you. Because if you continue like this, this 'glass wall' of yours will only get thicker and thicker, until you're unable to make any real connections, or even worse."

"I *am* coming back to my roots," Momo says. "That's why I moved out of LA, and—"

"You moved back to Senoia years ago. In that time, you've barely spent time with your parents." Dr. Heather tentatively wraps her arm around Momo's shoulder.

"I've known you since you were a teenager, Momo. I know what you had with Jireh and the gang, not even from you, or from... from Ayo, I've seen it first hand. When you guys would come to pick him up after each session, I could see it. You don't lose friendships like that. For your sake, call Jireh."

The rest of the session zooms by and a good deal more happens, but it's clear the primary piece of advice was for Momo to come back to the ground.

The gods and I follow her out of the office and into the street. We watch as people point and take photos of the disheveled celebrity, as if a peacock had escaped from the zoo and wandered out into the middle of the street.

She's stumbling through town, her hair a mess and her eyebrows scrunched up in thought. Still, people come up to her to ask for pictures and act like she slapped them in the face when she says no. As if it's impossible to imagine why anyone would want to halt their day just to meet the request of someone they have no connection to.

She's walking by a pet store when she stops for the first time and looks at an aquarium of goldfish placed by the window. For reasons beyond me, Momo starts laughing, loud and with wild abandon. Even still, there's no humor in it.

She places her finger on the glass, right over the fish near the top.

"Me," she whispers.

She then points to the one swimming at the side, and I sniffle. "Jireh."

A sob breaks through with a pang in my chest as she moves to the one eating something at the bottom. "Jonah."

I'm fully crying again when she gets to the last fish. It's being bought, and a worker, wondering why the hell Momo Sayuri is pointing at goldfish, gives her strange looks as she pulls it out.

"A—"

Momo gets up and leaves, but I don't follow her. Instead my feet just stand there looking at the fish, my vision getting blurrier and blurrier until I can't make out which fish is mine. My knees give out, and I think one of the gods places his hand on my shoulder, but I honestly can't say for sure. My brain and my heart and lungs spiral down and down and down, infinitely tightening until the pain all blurs together. Right here, right now, there's a million different paths I could cross, but there's no doubt in my mind that all of them will lead me to the truth: Jonah isn't the man under the tree. Jonah isn't the dirt.

I am.

HAVE

Some of the details are fuzzy, but if I remember correctly, the first time I placed a pair of scissors against my skin was my last day as a tenth grader. It came out of nowhere, like the answer to a question I never thought to ask.

Momo and the others had skipped their last periods, and since my phone died earlier that morning, I didn't see the group chat where they agreed to do so. They didn't know my schedule any more than I did theirs, so no one could come get me, so it was just me in the hallways at the end of school, wondering where the hell all my friends had fucked off to.

Said hallways were electric, though, with ecstatic teenagers barreling back and forth, shouting so many different names all at once that they all began to blend together. "Brandon" became "Lily" and "Tristan" became "Dwayne" and "Matthew" became "Erin" as names began to bang and crash into each other at the same pace that people banged and crashed into me.

Then it happened.

It wasn't the first time I'd experienced it, far from it. But this time was different in that I was aware of what exactly I was feeling. It wasn't just loneliness, it felt like I was watching a recording of a party I wasn't invited to. Like if I were to sink into the floors at that moment it would be the equivalent of someone dropping a pencil.

I stopped walking, and just stared at everyone. I wondered how they could be so carefree, how they could be so big, so much bigger than me, than that moment, than the world. With the way their hair billowed as they ran, the way their smiles widened as they flung their final papers into the air, and the way their eyes danced as they jumped on each others' backs on their way to the exit. They did it, and I did it, too. So what was the line between us for? Why was I constantly flickering, zapping in and out of existence, always needing people around me to feel like a person?

When I got home that night, I sat at my desk and just stared at the *Death Note* poster on my wall for quite literally hours. It was interesting because I'd almost never left myself alone with my thoughts before. I either hung out with friends, or watched, read, or listened to something. Hell, I'd sooner resort to busting a nut. But on that day, it was just me and the bitch in my brain.

And she told me vile, horrible things.

The names she called me, the way she looked at me, the way she made me look at other people, it made me so furious I felt I could spit.

So I did. Right on my desk. I remember just staring at that tiny pool of spit for what must have been at least ten minutes.

For some reason, this next part is crystal clear in my mind. I was tentative, scared of breaking myself, when I felt my fingers dig into the edge of the poster. Something in my jaw twitched, and I jerkily ripped it off the wall. It was a small act, but it felt good—really good. I don't know where the initiative to do it came from, but I ran into my bathroom and stared at myself in the mirror. Within seconds, more spit welled up in my mouth as I slammed my fist into the mirror. The glass didn't break, but it hurt like hell, and my brain loved it. It felt right, like scraping off dead skin or closing unused browser tabs. It felt like I was finally doing something right. I know it sounds pretentious, but I suppose the pain felt… righteous. Like this is what I was *supposed* to do when I felt this way.

My whole life, I had felt like shit for feeling invisible, but I saw something new that day: in my own little pocket of the universe, where no one could see or hear me, I could do whatever the fuck I wanted, whatever felt good.

I drew back my fist again, this time ready to actually break the glass, when I saw it. A pair of navy blue scissors peacefully resting by the sink.

The rest of what happened that day, I don't remember as clearly, just that it stopped being righteous and started hurting. A lot. As for the bitch in my brain?

I made her fucking day.

* * *

I either must've slept or passed out, because the next time my eyes open I'm laying on my back and there's so much light. Too much light. What the hell? Where am—

Oh. It all comes flooding back as quickly as it left, and a bitter wave rolls over me. Am I even on my back? Fuck, this white space is losing it's novelty, fast. I sit up, I think, and look to my left. The gods are looking at me like I might explode any minute. I don't hesitate to roll my eyes, folding my legs criss-cross applesauce.

"I'm not a bomb, you know," I say, wiping the imaginary dust off of my shorts. "I'm sorry I lost my cool. Won't happen again."

"Yes it will," God Two says. "It'll happen again and again, and not just because of your friends. There's an innumerable amount of heartache in the human story. Sometimes it's smaller than the joy, but it's almost always far louder.

"You're different now, Ayo. You aren't part of one of the longest, darkest, greatest stories ever told, you're a spectator of it. You can choose which pockets of it you get to watch. There's so much hope out there, so much laughter, and so much innovation! There's no reason for you to put yourself through this. I've said this before and I'll say it again: you got out!

"There are many other places to visit, many things to experience. You could go back to look at the pyramids when they were golden and white, or at roman sculptures when they were painted... Hell, you could go to 2052 when humans are finally able to upload their consciousness into game consoles! The whole world is yours, Ayo. Stop punishing yourself. You did enough of that when you were alive."

The world is mine? Why now? Why not when it mattered, when I was looking for something to *make* mine? Why wasn't the world mine when I stopped myself from falling in love with writing? Or all the times my father called me useless? Why wasn't the world mine when I jaywalked? Why now? Why fucking now?

"God Two," I say. "Why do people die?"

God Two visibly deflates and opens his mouth to speak, but God One beats him to it. "Because that's what makes life, life," he says.

I blink. "That's the dumbest thing I've ever heard."

God One shrugs and pulls a magical cigarette out of his ass. He then lights it and smoke magically comes out of his mouth when he puffs.

"Well how about you guys? Do you die, eventually? Like, after the sun swallows the Earth and the universe meets its end at the end of time or whatever, will you have a last day?"

The gods shake their heads.

I honestly can't help it. I begin to laugh, in perhaps the same way Momo laughed at the fishes. Chuckles snowball out of my mouth, so much so that when they erupt from my lips as cackles I'm sure I look like a mental patient. I've been so stupid, taking these guys seriously. They've been spectators their entire lives, so of *course* they don't understand. This sweet gig, this... privilege they've had, immortal beings who can watch all the sunshine and rainbows they want, with hundreds of years worth of stories to consume. They've got it good. They've never been made fun of, hit, or had to worry about anything other than leading whichever poor sap got clapped through this weird hodgepodge of an afterlife. Fuck these guys.

God Two quirks his eyebrows. "Did we say something humorous?"

"Fuck you! Both of you!"

God One's eyes narrow. "Excuse me?"

"You fucks just don't get it! You can't understand how shitty it is that life has stages, or that the best ones are the beginning! Why the hell is there even a beginning anyway?! Why is there an end? Why can't we just *exist*? What genius decided time would be a good idea? Which genius left things up to fate? You dumbasses sit here and tell me to get over it and go see the wonders of the world knowing my friends lives are in jeopardy? Knowing it was *my* carelessness that caused it?"

God Two reaches out to me. "Ayo, I understand how you're feeling, but it wasn't entirely your fault. Fate—"

I slap his hands away. My body isn't doing anything for me. "Don't. Don't you fucking dare. You guys don't understand shit. This is all just some game to you, right? Well it isn't to me, so the least you can do is not be condescending."

Every word is a bullet.

"Ayo, I know is must be hard, but you have to understand—"

I do something I've never done before. I tackle him.

The two of us tumble to the ground. I raise my fist and bring it down on the deity's face. No blood is shed, and I instinctively know he's choosing to get hit, but it feels good, so I do it again and again. A smile finds its way onto my face and I hit harder, wondering when the high of succumbing to my anger will die out, or even *if* it'll die out. Each punch fuels my rage and my rage fuels each punch, so it spins and spins and spins, until where I begin and where he ends no longer exist. My entire being exists just to attack and attack and—

There's a hand on my shoulder. I look over it and through the moisture in my eyes I can make out God One, looking at me with an expression I didn't think he was capable of making. His magical cigarette is nowhere to be found.

I jerk away from God Two and stare at my quivering hands. There's still no blood, but I've prided myself for so long on not being barbaric, for never letting my rage make me something that I'm not. I've never once raised my fist, not even in retaliation. Yet here I am, my hands mocking me, laughing at whatever I've become. I don't know, and I don't *like* who I am when I'm not with Momo, Jonah, and Jireh.

The lump in my throat tells me I'm about to start crying again when God One crouches in front of me and places his hand on my shoulder once more. He doesn't look particularly angry, but he's not exactly giggling, either.

"Ayo, you dumbass. Life is life *because* it's tiny. Immortality is far more meaningless than what you guys have. Even if you're like us, and you manage to give yourself a purpose, one that could, in theory, last for billions of years, eventually there will be nothing to grasp. Days will combine, and the past and the future will become redundant because emotions and memories will begin repeating themselves over and over again in one endless loop. The only reason your species has gotten this far isn't necessarily because they were smarter, it's because they fear reaching the end. They wanted to do as much, to live as much as they could, so they built skyscrapers, wrote bibles, and filmed billion dollar film franchises. You were bored, and you couldn't stand it, so you bent the world over backwards until it entertained you. That's on you guys, on your mortality—not on anyone else. You think we wouldn't give *anything* to have an end? There isn't enough spontaneity in anyone's existence to last forever.

"Look, in a way you're right. God Two—goddamnit I hate these stupid fucking names you've given us—God Two keeps trying to portray it as a gift, and while in some ways it is, I understand your dilemma. You're like us now. Forever floating, with all the power and time in your hands but none of the heart or ability to do anything with it. Not for long, anyway. But eventually you've gotta realize that humans die so they don't *have* to be God. Believe me or not, the way I see it, that's a gift."

I sniff. "Except you bring us here."

God One nods. "Except, unlike us, you can leave whenever you want."

"God One!" God Two gasps.

"It's true, isn't it? We might've trapped you, but it's the best of both worlds because it's temporary. You can experience anything you want, and you can vanish whenever you get bored. Seems like a sweet deal to me."

God One removes his hand from my shoulder and not-so-slyly rubs it on his jeans. "At least it would be, if not for the fact that you never got the chance to fully live out the human experience."

"What?"

"You died, Ayo. Before we could see what became of you, you died. Your story was cut short, and that is truly unfair. All the money, love, and joy you get when running away from death, you missed out on a huge chunk of that. And for that I'm truly sorry, but there's nothing that can be done."

I blink again. "That was extremely long-winded, and I'm still not even entirely sure what you're talking about."

God One shrugs and stands up, whipping out his magical cigarette again.

"Okay, then," I say, standing up as well. "I'll do you one better, asshole. Why do people die young? Why aren't I a miserable thirty-year-old like the rest of my friends?"

"I'm sorry it's like this, Ayo," God Two says. "We made rules and beings to abide by those rules. Anything that happens is either the fault of the humans or the rules."

"Fuck it," God One says, puffing out magical smoke rings. "I'll tell him."

"Are... are you sure?" God Two asks. "Why?"

He doesn't answer. "Listen, Ayo, we started this experiment with a seed. It banged and we left everything up to gravity and the like. Thus, this is the result. The original plan was to destroy the entire thing if it ever went off the rails, but we were careless, young, and overly excited, and we just let things run haywire. Even after humans came along, even after we realized they were almost as smart as us, we didn't intervene. This whole thing was just some kind of toy.

"But it stopped being that way after blood was shed because of something other than nutrition. By then we were too far in. We couldn't—we *can't* do much but watch. Again, I'm sorry, but there's no rooted reason why people die before they're ready. Things just happen and brakes don't stop in time. That's just the way it is."

"That's fucking bullshit," I say.

God One shrugs and wraps his arm around me. "Humans and gods alike, we're too far gone for it to be anything else, Ayo."

Happy

Needless to say, seeing your name on a tombstone is surreal. Like, I know that's me, and my skeleton is probably chilling in there, but I can also touch myself. Right now, I can ruffle my hair, pinch my cheeks... I could whip out my dick and start furiously masturbating if I wanted to. I wouldn't say I'm a hundred percent sure of my existence, but I'm so assured in the sensations of being alive that it's hard to imagine that a very unalive version of me is six feet below the headstone with my name on it. I contemplate snapping to my funeral so I could actually see them burying me, but quickly decide against it. Too real. Too real.

In front of my grave, Jireh stands in a black trenchcoat and fluffy sandals, sipping what I presume is coffee. Her hair is pulled into a messy bun and the bags under her eyes are multiple shades darker than the rest of her face, I guess that talk Hunter had with Sydney didn't go too well. Next to her is Momo, still in the same damn clothes and shabby hair she had in Jonah's place. She's crouched down, placing flowers by my grave, and it's hard to get a read on what her facial expression means. The aviators she's wearing certainly doesn't help, nor does the fact that it's minutes from being completely dark out.

"I don't understand Ayo," God Two says from beside me. "Why would you want to come here? It's—"

"Shhh!" I tell him. "This is important."

"Are you gonna say anything?" Jireh asks, eyebrow raised.

Momo sighs. "When the hell did you stop being so sweet?"

"Somewhere around when you hung up on me."

Another sigh. "Still holding on to that, eh?"

Jireh humorlessly laughs. "See you around, Momo."

She turns away and Momo pinches the bridge of her nose. "Stop. I'm sorry, I'm sorry."

Jireh keeps walking, not even bothering to look over her shoulder. "You've got a lot of things to be sorry for, I imagine."

"And you don't?" Momo asks, standing up.

Jireh stops. "Excuse me?"

"What? You gonna act like you're some saint? Like you didn't leave your brother to rot when he needed money?"

Jireh turns around and briskly walks towards her, stopping when her face is about an inch from Momo's, her fists clenching in her pockets.

"I can smell the whisky on your breath," she spits, "so I'm willing to stop myself from slapping you. But don't test me, Momo."

"Fuck you, bitch. You don't get a patent on being pissed."

"Pissed? Pissed at what, taxes? You're a fucking millionaire!"

"So?"

"So, you don't get to act like your life's a bitch when you can afford to buy three more!"

"Do you want my life?! Please, by all means, TAKE IT!"

"Oh, and all the bitchiness that comes with it? I'm good, thanks!"

"*I'm* a bitch? Me? Jonah was—"

"I gave Jonah money! I gave what I had and what I didn't, and in return he gave me jack shit. But since you brought it up, you must be feeling good about yourself, huh? Did you give him money when he asked because he said his rent had gotten higher or some shit? Did he tell you that Cassie told him to try some new expensive diet?

It's all bullshit, Momo. He just wants to feed the parts of himself that he never let grow up. It's the same shit you're doing. Lemme guess, the lights got too bright and now you want things to snap back to the way we were? We're not kids anymore. Eventually, you and Jonah are gonna have to accept that."

Momo sucks in her lips, presumably to hide the quivering. "At least I was there for hi—"

Jireh slaps her across the face. It's hard and fast, just like how she talks. The sound reverberates all over the cemetery, daring even a pin to drop.

"But you weren't there for me," she says. A tear slides down her cheek.

"Or my goddaughter." Momo gently places her palm against where she was slapped.

"You don't get to call her that."

"I know."

The two of them pause for a moment.

"JIREEEEEH!"

Momo lunges for Jireh, wrapping her arms around her. Tears stream down her face and sobs burst from her lips, quaking her entire body with each pulse.

"I'm sorry!" she cries. "I know I should've helped. I know I should've helped, but I was scared! It was just me in LA and the only people who wanted to talk to me just... I'm sorry, I'm sorry, I'm sorry, I swear! I'm sorry, I—" The rest of what she says is lost to her crying.

Jireh says nothing as she strokes Momo's hair and stares at my grave with an unreadable expression. A tear slides down her other cheek, and a small semblance of a smile finds its way onto her lips.

"Not so tiny now, are you?" she whispers.

I feel so pathetic that I can't help but laugh.

"What?" Momo croaks through broken sobs.

"Nothing, honey. It's okay. We all have demons, like how both of my baby daddies are deadbeats."

"Want me to send my guys?"

"You have guys?"

"I have four."

"Nice, can I borrow two?"

"Can I watch?"

"Bet."

Momo laughs tearfully and burrows into Jireh's red hair. "You still smell like a virgin."

Now Jireh laughs and it's like music to my ears. It's the first time she feels like the Jireh I remember, and her dancing eyes do nothing but make me wish I hadn't been a careless idiot even more.

Momo pulls away from Jireh and removes her shades to wipe away her tears. Despite being at least half a foot shorter, Jireh pats Momo's head.

"You ever gonna move back to LA?" Jireh asks.

"Permanently? I don't know if I ever want to, except for work, of course. Before I blew it was just a hotter, wetter Senoia, but after, it was like... the ocean."

Jireh's eyebrow raises again and her grin returns. "The ocean? You still can't swim?"

"I fail to see how that's relevant."

"Weren't you in a shark mov—"

"Hey."

"Hey."

"When was the last time you had jollof rice?"

Jireh blinks. "What?"

"You know, jollof rice, that orange rice Ayo's mom used to make for us."

"Oh, jollaw rice?"

"Yeah. It's actually pronounced 'jollof.'"

"Since when?"

"Since always, actually. We always mispronounced it and he always corrected us."

"Huh. I haven't had it since Ayo passed."

Momo grabs Jireh's shoulder. "There's a Nigerian restaurant in Atlanta, you down?"

Jireh blinks again. "You want to drive to Atlanta?"

Momo nods.

"Now?"

Momo nods.

"Why?"

"I don't know, I miss it," she says, shrugging.

Jireh gently pushes Momo's hands off of her and pulls her to her side.

"Sure, bud," Jireh says, placing her arm around the taller girl's shoulder. "That's what you miss."

The two stare at my tombstone for so long and with such intensity that an electric current runs up my spine, because for a moment it almost feels like they're looking directly into my eyes.

"No single snowflake is responsible for an avalanche, but if a snowflake is smart, it knows it can sit this one out and nothing will change," God Two says. I jump because I honestly forgot the guy was here.

"What the fuck does that mean?" I ask, tired of cryptic musings.

"It took Fritz Von Hugo several years to realize that 'nothing will change' doesn't exist. He was perhaps one of the most celebrated German soldiers in World War I. If there was anyone who could gather up fighters to rally against the Nazis, it would have been him, but he couldn't. When I asked him why, he said it was PTSD. And while that was probably true, I think he just got tired of gunfire, blood, and fighting for things bigger than himself. And even though he did mentally oppose the Nazis, he felt he could sit thay one out and a powerful resistance would rally on its own and resolve the crisis. Six million corpses later, he killed himself."

"You're doing that thing again where you think you're saying something but you're really not," I say.

God Two sighs. "You being there or not. Something will change. Something *always* changes. Even if we don't necessarily get to decide in which direction."

"Okay, fine," Momo groans, her gaze dropping to her feet. "I miss him. There. I said it. I still miss him. God, how long has it even been?"

"It's actually a little over ten years now," Jireh replies, gently rubbing her friend's shoulder.

"Then why do I still miss him?" Momo whispers.

"Because you're cursed with being human."

"Remember how anxious he would get at the drop of a hat?"

"Yeah."

"Or how his accent would come out at the most random times and we'd debate on whether or not to point it out?"

"Heh. Yeah."

"He was so precious, too. Always messing up but always knowing what to say to fix his stupid messes."

"Shit. Stop—"

"And so gentle. I remember one time I broke this computer thing he was building for a class he was struggling with, but he just laughed and went back to work."

"Momo..."

"He was so vulnerable, but he almost always put my bullshit in front of his bullshit. Always willing to help, even though he never felt capable. Oh! And he had like, the best smelling cologne I've ever smelled to this day!"

Now Momo and Jireh are both crying, looking at my stupid grave and burning something in my stomach in the process.

"Hey. Do you remember his obsession with Earl Sweatshirt?" Jireh asks.

"Oh yeah! I fucking hated that shit. He and Jonah would play it on repeat constantly and it was just this weird stoner sounding high out of his mind over these weird ass beats!"

"Jesus Christ I wanted to punch his stupid face every time he played that awful dreams song!"

"Ha! Oh, and remember how he would get super defensive whenever we tried to ask him when he was getting his permit?"

"He definitely failed that shit."

"Oh, one hundred percent!"

She's right. I did fail that shit.

"Fuck," Jireh sobs. "Why do you have me crying over him? I can go months without him crossing my mind."

Now it's Momo's turn to wrap her arm around Jireh. "Do you remember how he died? He was laggin' behind us, like always. I think he kept choosing to do that, 'cuz I don't remember pushing him away. I think he made the choice to always stay behind us."

"You're probably right."

"Yeah, I don't think he—"

"He didn't feel worthy."

Silence envelops the two again.

"Yeah."

"And look at us now," Jireh says with a jaded laugh.

Momo chuckles as well. "Yeah, he'd feel totally different if he could see our asses now."

No, Momo. I wouldn't.

"Shit," Jireh says, wiping her eyes, "I really miss him. Like hell. Why? Why do I wish he was here playing that stupid godforsaken dreams song all of a sudden?"

Momo laughs through her tears. "He told me about it, you know? How he didn't feel like he belonged. And you know what I did? I fucking *kissed* him. I kissed him! In no way did I have any intent other than to make him feel better in that moment. I didn't talk with him to process his feelings, I didn't ask him how I could help, I just fucking KISSED HIM!"

Momo's sobs take over her whole body until there's barely enough room left for words.

"I practically killed him," she says, barely audible.

Jireh wraps both arms around Momo and tightly hugs her as if she's trying to stop her from shattering into a million tiny Momos.

"Maybe we all did.".

No. No, no no, no, *no*! This is wrong, they can't possibly think by some bullshit, disjointed logic that this is *their* fault, right? I'm the dumbass who didn't see a monstrous truck hurtling towards him! How am I supposed to tell them that it was me? That they were the only things tying me down to Earth?

It's then that I notice the stars.

There are so few of them, scattered across the sky like broken shields, severed sentinels left to drift for eternity and watch what they can no longer protect. Momo, Jireh and Jonah rode their bikes into me and I popped their bubbles. The stars and the wind are no longer laughing with them, and I'm not there to fix it.

Instinctively, a rumble crawls its way up my throat. As tears blur my vision of the remaining stars, the rumble erupts from my mouth as a scream. It charges into the sky like fire, but can't ignite the stars like Jonah's could. So it stills to a float and waits to die.

But it doesn't—it *can't*, because Momo screams. Without warning, she pulls away from Jireh and screeches into the sky. It finds my cry and builds, and builds. It doesn't change the fact that the stars are gone, but it doesn't need to. The fire starts to become its own star, its own light, slowly and steadily setting the sky alight in a way the old stars never could.

Then Jireh joins in and control of the fire is wrestled from me. My throat burns as my scream dies, but Momo and Jireh do just fine without me. Their flames build, tongues of fire fueled by unwanted pregnancies and clout chasers, pain giving them the strength and protection that childhood could never—

Another scream joins in. It's unfamiliar, until I see him rise from the shadow of a tree. He's crying too, his scream chopped up by the spikes of his sobs and the jaggedness of his throat. It's raspy and weak, but it, too, has fire I can't deny. The sky dances, and dances, and dances.

It takes a while, but eventually the three of them quiet down, the job essentially complete. They have what they had back in high school again: each other.

Jonah seems to have tried for this meetup. His bird's nest is hidden under a faded black beanie, and he's practically swimming in the jeans and red flannel he's wearing. On his feet are actual sneakers, something I don't think he ever wore throughout his entire high school career.

"Holy shit! You actually came," Momo says, like she's seeing a dinosaur. "...I'm sorry. I'm sorry, I'm sorry, I'm sorry, I'm sorry, I panicked and—-"

"You're fine. I was... I'm being stupid."

The awkwardness builds until Momo does what Momo does best.

"So you're still thirstin' for my man, huh?"

The three of them laugh, but for Jireh and Jonah it feels like it's being shoved out of them. Not forced, exactly, more like the laughter you get when a character in a show or movie you hate makes a genuinely good joke. It snaps out of them and the two of them know it because their gazes snap to each others'.

"Jonah, how you feelin'?" Jireh tentatively asks.

"I've been worse."

"Yeah, I bet."

"I'm sorry," they say in unison.

Neither makes a move to hug or say anything more. They merely smile at the other and look at Momo, who grins widely and sits in front of my grave.

Jireh and Jonah follow suit, albeit with less enthusiasm.

"Just bought this damn trenchcoat and now you're making me get it all dirty with cemetery dust and shit," Jireh grumbles.

"Shhhh," Momo says. "I'll buy you a new one."

"You'll buy me three."

"I miss us," Jonah whispers. "I miss him."

"Yeah," Momo says.

"I loved how curious he was. Always wanting to learn as much as he could. So humble, almost to a fault."

Jireh chuckles sadly. "Definitely to a fault."

"And that thing he would do with his nose whenever he was thinking."

"Oh shit," Momo chimed in. "Teenage-me practically creamed herself every time he did that."

"Yeah, he was sexy like that."

Jireh shakes her head. "You guys need to get laid."

"Pfft, I get hella bitches," Momo retorts.

"Mhm, your on-screen kisses don't count."

"Shit. What about—"

"On screen sex scenes don't count either."

"Fuck! Okay, hear me out. If I were to—in theory mind you—say, blow a producer for a role, how does that measure up?"

"Then I'd say I'm happy you're not in LA anymore!" There's actual fireworks in Jireh's voice, and she almost sounds like little Sydney for a moment.

A nearby lamppost flickers out of life and the three of them are drenched in complete darkness. Judging by their sounds, none of them seem particularly bothered by it.

"Fuuuuck," Momo groans. "Help me out here, Jonah."

That right there is classic Momo. Noticing someone is being left out of the conversation and doing her best to bring them back in. A giggle bubbles its way out of my lips. Those are my fucking friends, man. And they're fucking alive. They don't need their youth to protect them anymore. They don't need *me*.

"Jonah?" Momo asks when he doesn't respond.

There's something wrong with his voice. "I'm sorry…"

"Jesus, Jonah," Jireh says. "Life's a bitch, and sometimes we do bitchy things because of her. But let's talk about all that shit later. Right now we can—"

"—but can I borrow some money?"

Pop.

Endings.

"Have you guys ever thought about how girls just have these random humps on their chest that's used to feed babies, and men just randomly decided that it was hot? Like, someone sat down and watched a grown woman breastfeed her baby and his dick got hard. At baby feeding. At *babies*. Holy fucking shit! Modern sexuality is an offshoot of pedophilia. We're all pedophiles! I'm a pedophile, you're a pedophile, my dad's a pe—"

"Shut up, Jonah," Past-Momo said, as she stepped out of her car with two boxes of donuts held under her arm.

"Please tell me you have plain," Past-me hollered. He was laying on his back, his body sprawled over the grass with his forearm draped over his eyes. Past-Jireh and Past-Jonah's backyard was massive, but had little to shade itself from Georgia's heat.

Past-Jonah leapt up and strode over to Past-Momo. "Just so you know, you're a pedophile."

"Congratulations! Now take these donuts so I can bother Ayo."

"Uh, what?" Past-me removed his arm from his eyes to look at her.

"Hush. Let me see your hair."

"Nooo…" he weakly crooned.

Past-Jireh shut the trunk as she walked across the massive driveway and headed towards them, a pack of beer barely held in each arm.

"Jonah, if Mom and Dad knew about this we'd be toast," she said, struggling not to fall while glaring at Past-Jonah, who made no move to help.

"Don't let your mind drift to the negative," Past-me said as his girlfriend did unspeakable things to his hair. "I heard that on a TED talk. Or in a hentai about a cheating midwife. Not sure."

God, I remember how scared I was back then, worried that my porn joke wouldn't go over well. Just watching me now you can see it in my eyes. Fear. So much fear. Constantly sweating over nothings that chased me further and further from home. It's odd; I almost never thought I'd come back to this time, but watching them now, watching *us* now, so full of light and tiny burdens, it almost seems fake. Like a layer of icing on a pile of shit. I don't want this version of us to be secondary to the one in ten years, but it gets harder and harder the more I watch.

"Definitely a hentai," Past-Jonah said, saving my ass. "Think I've even seen that one."

"Oh! Is it the one with the teacher?" Past-Momo asks.

"Yep," Past-Jona—no, Jonah said, sucking his fingers.

"Did you... Did you just steal a donut?" Jireh gasped.

"Yes."

"Bitch!"

"What?"

"We weren't supposed to start eating until Ayo was ready!"

"Why not?"

"It's not *your* birthday!"

"And?"

Jireh groaned and grabbed the boxes from Jonah, not forgetting to kick his shin before stomping away.

"You don't mind, right, Ayo?" Jonah asked Past-me.

"I'm in too much pain to mind," he said as Momo committed further war crimes on his head.

"You know, I like you, Ayo," Jireh said. "We used to have this one friend back in grade school, who would get upset at the littlest things. Never really been one to smack a bitch but I got close, let me tell you."

"Oh yeah!" Momo said, letting go of Past-Me's hair. "I remember her, she was so pretty! What was her name again? Shit... something like Bella, or—"

"Belinda," Jonah said, taking a swig of Past-me's birthday beer. "Last name was Mensoo or something, Ghanaians."

"Ah," Past-me said. "That explains a lot, Ghanaians kinda suck."

"They do?" Jireh asks.

"Yep."

Momo goes back to Past-me's hair. "Isn't that a little... racist?"

"Definitely. I'm allowed, though. Nigerians are given rights to be mean to Ghanaians. It's in the Bible. Check."

Jonah whipped out his phone and took another swig. "He's not wrong."

"Nice," Past-me said.

They fist bumped.

Jireh rolled her eyes and grabbed the can from Jonah. "That's for Ayo, dumbass."

"Okay, I know for a fact you just heard him say he didn't care like, two seconds ago."

"But *I* do."

"It's not *your* birthday, though."

"Die."

Jonah reached for the can. "I'm trying, but you took away my fucking beer!"

Jireh kept it out of his reach as she walked over to Past-me and crouched, giving him the can.

"Happy birthday, Ayo," she said with a warm smile.

Said smile immediately dropped when she turned back to Jonah. "Find something that'll do it faster!"

"Happy birthday, shitbag. Gimme my beer!" Jonah hollered, throwing blades of grass at me and flipping his sister off.

I took a swig with a shit-eating grin on my face and flipped the bird back at him. Jireh pointed and laughed as Jonah groaned and fell back on the lawn.

"Hey," Momo whispered.

I looked up at her. "Hey."

"I love you."

"I deeply prize and cherish your mind and body as well."

Chuckling, she kissed my forehead and went back to molesting my hair.

* * *

Ayo seems to snap back to reality, and with jerky movements he turns to... *sigh*. He turns to God Two (ugh) and shakes his head.

"Take me back to the white place, please. Take me back to the white place," he whispers.

God Two nods and snaps his fingers—an unnecessary theatrical thing he does because of "aesthetics"—and we're back in the void.

Without uttering a word, Ayo lies on his back and stares at nothing, taking shallow breaths and blinking sporadically, letting the silence get thicker and heavier for a bit too long.

"Uh... Ayo," God Two says, trying to alleviate the tension. "Where would you like to go next?"

He says nothing for a while, but eventually speaks. His voice is like molasses, though, dull and sluggish.

"Do my friends ever get better? Do they ever become like how they used to be?"

This is actually a question with a happy answer, so God Two is all smiles.

"Would you like to see for yourself?" he asks.

"No," Ayo says, killing God Two's buzz. "Them being happy wouldn't erase the bullshit I put them through."

Dick.

He stares at nothing for a few more minutes, repeatedly opening his mouth to speak but closing it right after.

"God Two?" he finally asks.

God Two is less enthusiastic about answering him this time. "Yeah?"

"Where the hell is this place?"

"This is the void, reality in its untampered form. Time doesn't exist here, and neither does matter. We had to add an artificial source of gravity, but other than that, this place is quite literally nothing."

"Huh. Neat. When Momo and Jonah and Jireh die, will I get to see them here?"

"...I'm afraid the void is too massive for you to ever reasonably cross paths. Unless you all choose to live forever, in which case it's inevitable... it's never happened before, though."

Ayo just sighs.

I conjure a cigarette as God Two approaches him and crouches by his head.

"Why does your death's effect on your friends surprise you so much? Didn't you know how much they loved you?"

Ayo shrugs. "Of course I knew they loved me, but there's more to life than love, right? The entire time we were friends I only took and took and took. I guess I always thought if my stupidity would ever catch up to me and kill me, at the very least they wouldn't have to be constantly slowing down to keep pace with me."

"But Ayo, you purposefully stayed behind them, that's why they didn't get hit by the truck in the first place."

"Jesus Christ, I didn't mean it literally."

"Perhaps neither did I."

The ungrateful shitbag sighs.

"Fuck off, God Two. The bottom line is that they don't need me. They should be fine. I mean, Jireh's moved on, but Momo keeps coming back to me and Jonah apparently turned to drugs instead of mourning, and now it's all gone to shit." He rubs his palms against his face. "This doesn't make any sense. They should be fine."

God Two opens his mouth to speak, but I've grown tired of him dancing around the subject. He needs to learn a lesson about brevity, for fuck's sake.

"Is that why you killed yourself?" I ask.

Silence.

I half expect Ayo to get mad again, or at least to cry or scream or some shit, but instead he just takes a long, deep breath, and says, "I always felt small with them, mainly because of how much I compared myself to them. But I stayed because I loved them and because the highs I got with them beat out the lows every damn time."

"So what the fuck happened?"

He pauses, as if to gather his thoughts.

"When we were crossing the street and their futures looked so bright and mine... fucking didn't, I guess I just felt so... so insignificant that the line between me being there and me not blurred. So I guess I... I don't know, maybe I wanted to prove it right or some shit, maybe I was daring God almighty for all I know, or maybe I was daring myself, maybe I was daring them, maybe I was going out of my fucking mind. God, it could have been the fucking liquid urine. Who the fuck knows?! All I know is that I stepped in front of that stupid truck!"

Now he's crying so hard that his back arches with each sob and his face twists tighter and tighter.

"And now I can't go back," he croaks. "That split second took it all away and I can't go back."

Despite all his episodes, I think reality is finally hitting him. The reality that he did all this damage and can't fix it. I can't relate to what he's experiencing, but I know it. I've seen it time and time again. Humans never realize how much power they have until they can't use it anymore.

"Can I?" Ayo whispers. He knows the answer. He knows that we know that he knows the answer, but he still asks. They always do.

"I'm sorry, Ayo," God Two says. "You can't go back."

He shuts his eyes and the bitterness behind each sob deepens. Each pulse hits his body with a tremor. He's crying for the same reason they always cry: because he only became powerless after he became God, and now there's nothing left to do or love or hate. No rope to pull or hand to hold. Now, with all the time and power in existence, he's truly tiny.

Ayo eventually softens his cries to slight hiccups and turns his head to God Two.

"I'm ready," he says.

God Two looks at me with moisture in his eyes and I shrug, igniting my cigarette and placing it in my mouth. Again, and again. We see it again and again, but each time he bleeds for them.

"Are you sure?" God Two asks, turning to Ayo.

He nods. "I want to go back to graduation day. At the ceremony."

God Two sends me another worried glance. He doesn't flick his fingers this time.

* * *

God Two shifts us to the backstage of our school's auditorium, where I'm standing in front of a mirror trying to adjust my graduation cap.

I watch myself for a few seconds, resisting the temptation to rip that awful hat off my head, spin me around, and tell me to run. Run as fast as I can away from all these people, from these places, from all of it.

But even if I could, it wouldn't fix anything. I know by now that people can't fill empty footprints that easily.

So instead I meet Ayo's gaze. He can't see me, of course, but I see him, and for me, that's all that matters.

"H-hey Ayo..." I croak. My throat is hoarse, so I clear it.

Take two. "Ayo. It's me. I'm... I'm sorry. Shit. Fuck, shit this is so fucking stupi—"

I sigh.

Then I sigh again.

"I'm sorry. I'm sorry we're so dumb, and I'm sorry we keep looking for others to not feel dumb. I'm sorry about the time we drank a bit too much hoping we'd vomit and Momo would stop talking to that douchebag Bryce and come help us. I'm sorry for staying up past midnight writing and rewriting that stupid poem, only to end up scrapping the whole thing. I'm sorry we never helped each other, I'm sorry we were so scared of each other. I'm sorry for always asking for Jonah's help with calculus instead of just trying it ourselves. I'm sorry for that time we cried in front of everyone in the fifth grade because Sarah Hall called us fat. I'm sorry we always looked in the mirror and always grimaced. I'm sorry we never let ourselves get good at anything, I'm sorry we always compared ourselves to others without giving us the chance to get better.

"I'm... I'm sorry for the marks on your thigh. That one's my fault, and it's not going away any time soon. At least not in any way that matters."

"Ayo!" Momo's voice called out, snapping both of us out of our daze. "You coming?"

"Yeah, on my way!" Ayo gives up on the hat and goes to stand behind her in line.

I follow him, still speaking to him as we walk.

"Your whole life, your *whole fucking life* you only defined yourself in comparison to others. Don't you see how that's bullshit?

Collectively, the line starts moving—quickly, I might add—to the stage.

Speed walking, I keep pace with Ayo.

"Even with that stupid metric, you still have worth! The future is literally different because *you* aren't there! And forgetting about others, there had to have been something, man. There had to! You're a human being! I don't have any answers for you, but you're just as complicated and bullshit ridden as the rest of them. You would've found your thing, but you never let yourself! It's almost like you didn't want to be proud of yourself, so you lied, and you lied, and you lied, but only to yourself!"

They've received their diplomas, and now they're facing the applauding and whooping crowd. Camera flashes from elated parents and applause from disobedient families like mine bounce around the hall, but I don't let it distract me. I'm very aware of the gods behind me and what I did and didn't ask them to do.

"The problem wasn't that you were invisible to them, it's that you were invisible to yourself. You wouldn't let yourself be anything other than a sidekick, so you kicked yourself because you hated being a sidekick. You hate yourself and you don't believe you deserve anything other than to hate yourself and it's bullshit, Ayo. You need to say it. You need to look in the mirror and say I love—

HI.

It's been a little over a year since I finished the first draft of *Our Bubble of Stars*.

I began this novel when I had just graduated high-school. I went to a small private Christian school, meaning I was parting ways with some people I had known since kindergarten.

At that point in my life, the question of who was I when I wasn't surrounded by others is one that absolutely terrified me. Yet, despite the fact that I still have no answer to this question, when I read *Bubbles*, I see a Tosin I no longer recognize. A Tosin who was yet to understand just how much bigger the world was, and how much more empathy he'd need before he could embrace it. That Tosin was stubborn, and lonely, and angry, and cynical, and somehow even more pretentious than me. He and I would absolutely throw hands if we ever met, but regardless, he and I thank you for reading this book, and look forward to creating even more sad kids.

For the obligatory quote:

> *Until we get old, there's water in the flowers, let's grow.*
> —Mac Miller
> *Surf*

About the Author

Tosin Balogun has always had itchy hands (do not take this line out of context). Ever since he was a kid he scrambled to create whatever he could, whenever he could, wherever he could, much to the horror of his parents.

He eventually found a home in writing, to which he swiftly became addicted to. He is currently studying computer information systems in Georgia State University with a minor in creative writing.

You can find him on Instagram @tosin_is_hungry and Twitter @tosin_is_hungry... also.

Thank you for reading a MoonQuill original novel. To experience more exciting stories, visit us at MoonQuill.com

To know when we release new books, join our mailing list from our site and receive three books for free!

We will never spam you!

To talk with other members of the MoonQuill community, check out our community Discord.

Finally, we would really appreciate it if you could take a moment to review the book. Every review greatly helps the author and supports their ability to continue writing fantastic books for us to enjoy.